fragments of hope

PIERCED HEARTS

BOOK TWO

VIOLET HAZE

STOKED PUBLISHING HOUSE

Originally titled *Stripped To You*

Cover Design from Designs By Dana
Stoked Publishing House

ISBN-13: 978-1-7355302-3-9

spoiler alert!

Please be aware, while this story may be read as a standalone, reading Fragments of Us first is best.

The first scene in the first chapter of Fragments of Hope will contain a **huge spoiler** from the ending of Elizabeth's novel of which Yvette is an important part in. This novel will also continue many storylines from the first book.

Unless you don't mind being lost at first as to who's who, or ruining the ending of the previous novel, my recommendation is that you get to know everyone from the beginning!

Happy Reading! :)

chapter one

THERE ARE SOME THINGS IN LIFE YOU NEVER FORGET.

You never forget the day the love of your life died.

The day your mother sold you to a stranger so she could get her fix.

The day you were adopted.

And finally, the day you honestly believe nobody will ever love you.

Don't get me wrong—I'm incredibly lucky.

I'm lucky I escaped the man my mother traded me to when I was ten.

Fortunate to have been taken in by the Pierce family.

Blessed to later have that same beautiful and loving family adopt me, treating me as if I belonged.

But the truth is, I've never felt like I fit in with them.

And I did the most stupid thing a girl in my position could do — I fell in love with a man who would never be mine.

I kept my love to myself for many years.

Anybody who knew Stefan loved him and I'm no different.

I'd just been a young girl when I came to live with Stefan and his family. I was one of the lucky ones and I knew it. Most people didn't take in children my age. They all wanted babies.

I definitely hadn't been a baby. I'd been a girl on the verge of puberty who'd narrowly escaped being assaulted by a nasty man who had traded my mother drugs for me. A girl who hadn't known what being loved felt like, but wanted so badly for these people she now stayed with to love her.

The moment Stefan smiled at me, though, joy had filled me. He'd had such a lovely smile that I fell in love with him in that second. It was the day I first came to stay with him and his family — and the feeling only intensified over the years.

I loved him through his relationship with Elizabeth and their break-up. I was there for him after he found out from Grace that their one night of sex had ended up with her getting pregnant. Then Elizabeth had come back into his life and I knew for sure there would be no chance for us.

In truth, there never had been.

Yet I couldn't help how I felt.

I never saw Stefan as my brother, even after I'd officially been adopted and became a Pierce myself.

Yes, I'd been a young girl, but I hadn't been blind. And I definitely hadn't been immune to feeling things for an older boy who'd treated me like the most precious person in his life.

I know Stefan had treated everyone the same way. He'd been kind, loyal and always a gentleman. Even after Elizabeth had broken his heart, he never spoke badly of her and I'd been so jealous. And angry; mad for him, for how she made him feel, and for my inability to be what she'd been to him.

He just saw me as his sister and after I kissed him one

Christmas under the mistletoe, there'd been no thinking otherwise. He never said a word, never treated me differently, and yet I knew. Without a doubt, I knew there would never be an 'us' but that didn't stop me from loving him.

If anything, I just loved him more.

But the day he died… that had been the worst.

That day had put an end to my illusion something would ever happen between us.

And now I'm forced to live without the one person who had given me something to look forward to as a little girl. He hadn't known it and I'd never told him, but his smile had changed my life.

Because, in it, I saw there truly was kindness and love in the world, and it could be mine if I just reached for it.

But I knew now, everything like that is one big lie.

If the world can take someone incredible like Stefan from me, it will take everybody else I love too.

So I, Yvette Renee Pierce, decided then and there while standing in the hospital and knowing he would never smile at or laugh at me just one more time, that I would never love anyone else ever again.

The thing is, the universe doesn't care about the promises we make to ourselves.

And I have a feeling it's going to make me eat my words because that's what the world does.

It's been one year, six months, ten days, twelve hours and forty-one minutes.

I've always told myself that I'll never be one of those people who counts time after a momentous tragedy—as if doing such a thing makes it easier to get through the day.

But I am one of those people. And it doesn't make it easier to get through the day; instead it just reminds me of the day my heart shattered and I swore I'd never love again.

I think anyone who has truly loved someone knows what it feels like when you lose those particular people. Whether they died or they walked away or something else happened, the pain of losing someone you love is unbearable.

At least, it has felt that way for me since he died and continues to feel that way, the ache never lessening.

For many months after Stefan's death, there were lots of moments where I did nothing except cry. My pain couldn't be contained and nobody tried to tell me I shouldn't feel the way I did, but nothing they said comforted me either.

Penny, my sister, attempted to be there for me and I appreciated her efforts. She's always been very kind and even though she offered to let me stay with her for as long as I wanted, I didn't want her to smother me either.

Then Elizabeth did something so kind I couldn't stay angry with her for breaking Stefan's heart all over again when she chose Simon instead. She came over just a few weeks after his death and offered to let me stay in the house given to her after my mom's death for free. It's the same house that would've been Stefan's if he hadn't insisted it be given to 'his Ellie.'

So that's where I've been living. I've spent the last year living off the money my mom, Liliana, left me when she died. Her death followed by Stefan's really shook the foundation of my life. Losing two people from the family who chose me so closely together makes me want to hide in my room and never come out.

But, of course, I can't do that.

Life goes on whether we want it to or not.

And that's what my life has taught me. I have to keep going and keep getting up every time I'm knocked down no matter how much it hurts.

So six months ago, I finally got a job at the local hospital, which will put my nursing skills to good use.

At first, working there had been difficult since it's where Stefan had been pronounced dead; where I went crazy on my family, accusing them of being the reason Stefan died, even though I knew better deep down.

And although I hate the phrase 'time heals all wounds,' it seems a bit true in this case. Or perhaps a part of me recognizes the hospital had been just the smallest portion of it all and so now, when I walk through the doors, it's just where I work.

The hospital's a fairly big one considering its location and barring specialty surgeries, we're able to take care of nearly everyone who comes in for help. And I work in the emergency room, which is where a good majority of the patients start, giving me the opportunity to assist various people.

Walking through the main doors, I head to put my coat and purse away, noticing as I pass by that Jenny is working triage this evening. It's seven on the dot when I clock in, and I work until seven a.m. I quickly assess the situation I'll be working in tonight: five patients in the waiting room, three inpatient rooms, two nurses on staff not including Jenny, and Doctor Hawkins.

Although everyone calls him Max — short for his full name,

Maximilian — when not around patients, I don't. I'm not comfortable with referring to Doctor Hawkins or Doctor Worthington with their first names, although that doesn't apply to the nurses. I think if they weren't both intimately acquainted with my breakdown in the ER all those months ago that they'd think me a snob. However, they both know and accept my reluctance to call them by their first names. I don't want to be close to a man in any capacity, ever again.

"Nurse Pierce."

Speaking of Doctor Hawkins, I turn on my heel as he speaks from behind me, looking straight up into his twinkling blue eyes. He shoves a hand through his hair, hair which is quite frankly too beautiful for a man, with its medium brown tone and glimpses of red and blond highlights throughout — and smiles at me while referring to me in the same manner I do him. It seems to amuse him and I know he does it because I refuse to use his first name; in fact, he calls every other person at the hospital by their first name.

As for his smile, I don't return it; instead, I lift a brow and wait for him to continue.

"How are you?"

Caught off guard by his question, a lift of my shoulders makes it crystal clear I have nothing of interest to share. I don't understand why he wants to know, or why he cares, but I answer him anyway. "Fine." After a brief pause, I feign interest in him due to my need to do the polite thing. "You?"

"Great!" He lifts the chart in his hand until my eyes are on it, then puts down his arm, and nods at a spot behind me. "Ready?"

"Of course," I reply with a sigh of relief, and he walks past me toward the room with the patient, making me glad he realizes I'm not interested in making small talk.

For a few minutes following, I wonder why he even asked, but then brush it off, thinking him merely being polite since we work together all night.

And with that, I shove it from my mind completely, focusing on the one thing which truly matters to me: my work.

chapter two

MY ROUTINE EVERY DAY IS THE SAME, EVEN WHEN I DON'T work. Being an evening person, I always work night shifts and prefer it that way.

So I get off work, head home, sleep from about eight a.m. to two p.m., then get up and do whatever I need to do before work. Usually, it's errands such as going to the bank or going shopping. If it isn't an errand, I spend my time reading, catching up on my DVR'd shows, or spend time with my family.

Today, as I roll over and turn off my alarm clock, it'll be getting a shower, followed by going to do my weekly grocery shopping since it's Saturday, and returning home to put them away. Once that's done, I have the evening off so I'll relax with some reading, and perhaps go see my sister Penny.

Sliding out from my warm, comfy bed, I head for the shower and the clean start to the day it will give me. Forty-five minutes later, I'm standing in the fruit section of the grocery store, trying to find a few perfect peaches to take home with me. That is, until I look up and discover Doctor Hawkins lifting his gaze from where he studies the apples a mere few feet from me, and his eyes meet mine.

"You don't want that one," he says, nodding at the peach in my hand without looking away. "It's bruised."

Taking a glance at it, I realize his observation is correct, but instead of putting it down, I lift a brow and cross my arms, the peach grasped tight in my fingers. "I would've noticed if you hadn't distracted me. I do know how to buy peaches, y'know."

"I'm sure you do." He puts down the apple he's holding and slides his hands into the pockets of his khakis while walking toward me. His lips curve up a little at the corners as if he wants to grin but is keeping it in check. "How're you?"

"That's the second time you've asked me that question and it's not even been twenty-four hours. Why?"

He stops a few inches from me, as if he's making sure not to touch me but wants to stand as close as possible. "Because you seem…" He pauses as if unsure whether or not he should continue, then shrugs as he finishes with, "lonely. And despondent."

Eyebrows rising in surprise at his words, I scowl at him, uncrossing my arms to put the peach back in the bin, then turn on my heels and walk away. Of course, he follows me seconds later and as I stop to put some yogurts in my basket, he gets some as well.

"It's none of your business whether I'm lonely or not, Doctor Hawkins." There's a bite to my words and they are intentional because I want him to get my point, and get it immediately. "We work together. Nothing else."

As I go to turn and walk off once more, he grabs my basket and tugs me back until I toss him a nasty look. "What part of that did you not get?"

"Oh, I got it." He smiles at me, unperturbed by my attitude, and continues to hold onto the basket so I can't leave. "But what if I wanted us to do more than work together?"

My answer is quick and succinct. "Not interested. Ever."

"Ouch." He laughs, the sound so deep and husky, a part of me I refuse to acknowledge responds in an undesirable way. "You don't even know what I was going to suggest."

"If it involves spending more than the hours at the hospital together, the answer is no. Forever."

His eyes search mine as if he's trying to determine whether I'm serious or not, and after a moment he lets go of the basket with a smile. Placing his hands on the front of his cart, he moves it, walking past me and going over to the eggs without another word. But just as I'm about to let out a sigh of relief, he leaves the cart there and comes back over to me.

"You see, here's the thing." I want to roll my eyes at him, but don't, making a 'what now?' face instead as he continues with whatever he wants to say. "On Saturday afternoons and Sunday mornings, I volunteer at this group home in the city, and I was hoping you'd join me."

Well, I didn't see that coming. Blinking at him, it takes me a moment to process what he's said, and of course, I feel foolish for assuming he wanted something romantic.

"Oh. I see." Chewing on my lip, I look down at my basket, then back up at him with a sheepish smile. "What time?"

Lifting his wrist, he cuts his gaze away from mine and takes a glance at it, before looking up at me once more. "It's five after three. I arrive at four-thirty and stay about an hour."

"I'm not even finished shopping. And I'll have to go home to put stuff away. Perhaps next time?"

"Sure." He doesn't sound as if he believes I will ever go but pulls a card and pen out of his pocket, scribbling on the back of it before handing it over to me. "Here's the address in case you change your mind. Or for next time."

"Thank you."

"I think you'd really enjoy it." He takes a step back and nods at me. "Have a nice evening, Yvette."

And with that, he walks over to his cart and disappears out of sight. The fact he calls me by my given name for the first time ever is something I realize a second before I take in the address on the card. This is followed by me having trouble catching my breath as I realize where he volunteers.

Which is the group home where I briefly stayed before the Pierce family took me in.

WHEN I PULL up to the group home, it's already five. I know Doctor Hawkins will be surprised to see me, but after he had left, I finished shopping, went and put the groceries away, then headed this way.

Although he said this place is in the city, it's actually a little outside it.

It looks different than I remember, but it's also been thirteen years since I've been here. Liliana had been the one who discovered me walking in town and once she knew I came from the city, she'd asked me how I made it an hour out of town. I never told her it was because I hitched a ride after escaping the man my mother had traded me and got out of the car when the couple who picked me up stopped to get gas. I figured the fact I escaped an evil man would be bad enough to explain and although what I'd done had probably saved my life, getting into a car with strangers hadn't been too smart.

However, I was ten at the time and rather panicked, so I forgave myself the poor judgment and never accepted a ride from another stranger again.

Anyway, after she took me home with her, the police were called and after they'd gotten all the information they needed, I'd been sent to the group home. I stayed there until Liliana could get everything in order so she could foster me. It had taken a good bit and during that time, I mostly kept to myself at the group home.

I don't remember much about it, but I do recall how kind everyone had been, and in complete honesty, I came today because I'm a little curious about what Doctor Hawkins does here as a volunteer.

Getting out of my car, I shut the car door just as the front door of the home opens and he walks out, along with three teenage boys who follow him. Catching sight of me, he grins, turning to the boys to say something before walking toward me.

Although it's early December, the weather has been pretty mild so far. It's fifty-eight degrees, with a whisper of a breeze and the sun shining bright. None of them wear a jacket, unlike me. Instead, they're wearing t-shirts of varying colors and designs, jeans, and tennis shoes. Doctor Hawkins fits right in with them, having changed from his outfit in the store to jeans and a dark blue polo.

He stops in front of me, our bodies a breath apart, and leans in to whisper, "Work with me. These kids think you're my girlfriend; I'll explain later."

"What?" I keep my voice low but bring my head back a little for some space, my eyes going wide. "You'll explain now."

"They've been here about a year now each. Brothers. They are thirteen, sixteen, and seventeen. Been bounced around a lot since they were taken from their parents four years ago. They have a hard time believing their lives will ever get any better since they live here now. I want them to see it's not true."

"What does this have to do with me?"

I don't mean to sound like a bitch, but I don't understand why him having a girlfriend makes a difference.

He doesn't take offense, though, at least from what I can see, as the corners of his mouth curve up in a ghost of a smile. Then, I feel rather than see him slide his hand down the side of my body until he clasps my hand in his, squeezing tight. "I spent four years here before turning eighteen. I want them to know I've got a great life in every way, and they fear no girl will want to date them."

Hiding my surprise at learning he lived in the system, I bite back my initial desire to remark that apparently no girl wants to date him if he's single. But, then I glance at the boys, who look at both of us, their eyes round with interest as they did so. I can only guess it's because he's holding my hand in his and they can't believe it, so I continue to speak softly as I respond. "Okay, but you're not going to kiss me in front of them are you?"

Surprise flares in his eyes even as he shakes his head. Then, keeping his voice level equal to my own, he states, "I only kiss someone if they're my actual girlfriend." His eyes sweep me from head to toe before his gaze returns to mine, glinting with amusement and definite interest. "For now, it's something I'll leave you looking forward to."

His words makes me want to yank my hand from his grasp, glare at him with all the contempt I feel at his assumptions about what will happen between us, and leave him looking like a fool in front of those kids. But the other part of me knows what it's like to feel so unwanted, and unlovable. And that part of me means I'll go along with him for this visit because these kids deserve hope in a world where they truly feel as if they have none. Even if I am miserable most of the time, I have no desire to disillusion them before their own lives will most likely do it for them.

When I don't take my hand from his, he must take it as permission to continue, which I guess it is. He tugs on my hand and starts walking, so I stay beside him and plaster a smile on my face as we stop in front of them a few seconds later.

From youngest to oldest, he introduces me. "Yvette, this is Peter, Vincent, and Paul."

I tamp down a laugh at realizing their names are all those of saints and nod at them. "Hi."

Paul scowls at me, Vincent gives a small smile in response, and Peter goes all wide-eyed before looking away from me.

"Wow, she's beautiful, Max," Peter says. "You did a good job."

"Thanks. I grew her all by myself."

They all laugh at that and I can't resist a smile of my own as he finally releases my hand.

"Let's shoot some hoops," he says, taking the basketball from Vincent's hands and walking backward. "You can join if you want, Yvette."

"Oh." I hold up my hands and shake my head. "Absolutely not. I'm into many things; sports isn't one of them. I'll just watch."

"That's okay. I've always wanted an attractive girl as my personal cheerleader."

"Who says I'll be cheering for you? Peter looks like he needs it the most, being the smallest and youngest."

Peter giggles, his brothers joining in with a visible relaxation in their stances at the same time, and all three of them throw me huge smiles before walking to take their place on the court.

Turns out, Peter's short stature works in his favor, along with his quickness because he makes score after score while the others don't fare so well. He weaves in-between and around them with what can only be described as finesse, and it's clear they are all trying to stop him from scoring but fail repeatedly.

I study each of them, and I have to admit, my eyes linger when they land on Doctor Hawkins. He's the tallest in the group and I find it hilarious a small, fast teenager outplays him with such ease. Well, by all of them actually, and who would've thought he would need my cheering more than three kids? Not me.

When he catches me looking at him, he winks and flashes a grin before saying, "All right boys, I've got work this evening so I have to get going."

A chorus of drawn out awe's follow his statement, but he tosses Paul the ball and hugs them goodbye one by one. After, they turn to me, waving with their big grins and run off inside, leaving me alone with him.

"Come on," he says with his hand extended toward me. I give his hand a wary look as I stand, and he laughs, wiggling his fingers. "I'll walk you to your car. Take my hand; they'll be watching."

"Don't believe in 'Thou shalt not lie'?"

"I believe in stretching the truth when it comes to showing some depressed kids that life isn't all bad." He steps closer and snatches my hand up in his, lifting it to his mouth to kiss the back of it before whispering, "Just for them."

Then, before I know what he's doing, he leans in and presses his lips to the corner of my mouth for a mere second before pulling away.

"And that," he says with a grin. "That was just for me."

I swear I suck in a breath and stop breathing from the tingling sensation his small peck sends shooting through me. A feeling I want nothing to fucking do with in any way. Along with the smile on his face and the twinkle in his eye, the way he makes me feel right then pisses me off because I can't make it stop.

So I tug my hands from his, nod and hurry back to my car as if he is chasing after me.

He isn't.

Instead, he stands rooted in place as I start the car and back out, watching me the whole way with his hands slipped casually in his pockets and the smile I want to smack off him plastered on his face.

chapter three

WHEN I KNOCK ON THE DOOR LATER THAT EVENING, PENNY answers with her usual smile of happiness and soft voice, stepping back to let me in automatically. "Yvette! I wondered when you'd show up."

Holding up the bags, I force a smile of my own and say while stepping inside, "I thought Chinese sounded like a good idea for dinner so I stopped on the way here."

"Sounds great!" She shuts the door behind me and takes one of the bags out of my hands. "Come into the living room and tell me why that smile of yours wasn't genuine, and why you'd try to pretend like it was to me of all people."

Ah, Penny. Not that I will admit it out loud, but out of all my siblings, she's my favorite. Even-tempered, fair, patient, kind, and super loving. It doesn't get better than her for a sister because she is so non-judgmental and even though she hadn't liked my treatment of Ellie, nor had she condoned it, she also understood.

Especially when she found out why I'd acted the way I had.

"Love is blind," she'd told me after Stefan had died,

hugging me against her when we were alone, with both of us crying our eyes out. "It doesn't care about what's proper, or what other people will think. Hell, in some ways, it's the most dangerous feeling because it's one not many have the power to control once it's hit them. It sometimes will consume you until you're doing or saying things you shouldn't."

"I don't know," I had sobbed to her, lifting my head to look into her eyes with a small laugh. "It made me crazy, Pen. You're in love, why aren't you acting crazy too?"

"Oh honey, I'm just better at hiding my crazy, that's all."

We both had laughed, and while everything wouldn't ever be the same without Stefan, I knew I'd be okay with having Penny as my support. And of course, I'm hers, along with our other siblings.

Only thing is, nobody in the family knows who Penny's love interest is. They've been together almost two years but she hasn't said a peep, and nobody's seen her with anyone. It's driving us all batty, but she insists that while it's serious, she wants to make sure it is for the long haul before she introduces us.

All we can think is, isn't two years pretty damn long? But, it's her life, and all we can do is wait for her to tell us.

Stepping into the living room, she places the bag on the table and then takes a seat on the couch. Once I put mine on the table next to hers and take a seat in the chair to her left, we both begin pulling out containers and setting ourselves up without another word.

Of course, once we're all finished doing that and consuming our food at leisure, she gives me an expectant look. "Well? Tell me what's going on, Yivvy."

Her use of my nickname from when I first came to live with

the family has my eyes tearing up. She only uses it when she knows it's something I don't want to share, but will anyway because it's her I'm speaking with. And she's the one I trust the most.

"You know the doctor I work with most of the time? Hawkins?"

"The hot one with the electric blue eyes you ogle all the time? Yeah. Why?"

My mouth drops open, but I quickly snap it shut before replying, "I do not ogle him!"

She rolls her eyes, eating a bit more before continuing. "Whatever. You do. And who could blame you? He's practically model material." When I scowl at her going on about him, she laughs. "Anyway, what's he done to upset you?"

"Uh, let's see." Setting down the container, I hold up a hand and count on my fingers. "First, he started being real nice to me at work last night, asking me how I am and shit. Then this morning, he gets up in my personal space in the store and invites me to volunteer at a group home with him. He gives me the card, only for me to realize it's the home I was living in before I came to live here. That's second. And third, I wanted to see what he did there, so like an idiot I went and he had me pretend to be his girlfriend to show these three boys there was life after the home. And dammit, it was good, only he ended up kissing me on the mouth." Flattening my mouth in a grim line, I lift a hand, pointing to where he put his mouth on me with one quick stab of my finger.

Penny stares at me wide-eyed, laughing the moment my eyes meet hers, and she sits down her container before throwing her arms up in the air. "That's great! Did you have fun?"

"No!" I shrug, giving her a massive sigh along with an eye

roll of my own as she laughs even harder. "Yes. I mean, other than wanting to punch him for putting his lips on me, I found out he lived there for a while when he was a teenager."

"Well," she says, sobering from her laughter with a deep inhale of air as she wipes the tears from her eyes. "Obviously he likes you, silly."

"I know, but I don't want him to!"

"You don't get to decide if he likes you or not; only if you like him back."

"I don't."

She actually fucking giggles and shakes her head before smiling at me real big. "Okay, if you say so."

"I do." I cross my arms over my chest and glare at her even more because she's just looking at me like she doesn't believe me. "Aren't you supposed to be on my side?"

"Come here." She taps the couch with her demand, so with a wary look on my face, I take a seat beside her. She immediately puts her arm around my shoulders and strokes my hair like the mother figure she's become to me since Stefan and our mom died. As I cuddle into her side, she speaks in a soft, sweet tone. "I am always on your side, but it's been over a year and a half since Stefan died. And while I know how you felt about him, I don't want you to be depressed forever. If you like someone, you should find out where it can go."

I feel my eyes start to water, pain filling my chest at her words, and I hate it. I can't manage to prevent the sniffles as a tear slides down my cheek.

Penny squeezes my shoulders in an attempt to comfort me. "I miss him too, Yivvy. We all do. But life goes on whether you want it to or not. And I wish you wouldn't be so afraid of it or scared to let someone else in."

"How do you know what I'm afraid of?"

The words are barely a whisper, but it's apparent she heard me when I feel and hear her soft sigh before she responds. "It's written all over your face. Plus, I'm your sister. You've been in my life a long time now. I might not've known about your feelings for Stefan, but I knew you were love sick over someone. I guess I just never expected it to be him and that's the only reason it caught me off guard. And now, when we're out and about, you get this mixed look of envy and disgust all in one on your face, and I know it's because you wish you had it."

"It's not fair." Childish thing to say, and I know it, but it isn't dammit.

"Of course not. Nothing is really ever fair, sis. But it's how you deal with it that matters. And locking yourself away, on the inside or in your home, isn't healthy. If you want to be alone because that's truly what you desire, then stay single. But I know that's not what you want, and you can't be afraid to try because the person might leave you. Death is inevitable for all of us, so you should enjoy the time you have."

"It's not just death Pen. It's being left at all. It's losing the people I care about over and over. I'm not sure I could handle it."

"You've done it quite a few times haven't you? You're stronger than you give yourself credit for. And while you can't control what others do, you also can't let fear keep you from getting what you want and need."

I know she's right in my head, but convincing my heart of the truth in her words won't be so easy. My heart has always ached for something I knew I would never have—Stefan—and I'm not sure it knows how to desire anything else.

But I recall the way Doctor Hawkins' kiss made me feel,

and even though it really had been a friendly goodbye kiss more than a sexual one, I'm not blind. He likes me, has shared a private part of his life with me, and has made it clear he has every intention of dating me if I'll let him.

I'm just not sure I'm ready.

And I'm not sure I ever will be.

THE FOLLOWING evening I return to work, relieved to know I'll be working with Doctor Worthington because Doctor Hawkins has the night off. I'm not ready to see him, which makes me hate the fact I even care about whether I do see him or not, since I don't want to feel anything about him at all. What I need is to rewind and make the choice to not go to that group home; then he wouldn't have kissed me and I wouldn't be riddled with anxiety for over a whole day now.

But it turns out my whole evening will go to shit in a rather unexpected way.

"Yvette," Doctor Worthington calls out to me with a smile as I approach the nurses desk. "It's been a busy day which means it's sure to be an eventful evening." He holds up a couple patient folders, extending them out to me. "These are the patients waiting. Read through them real quick so when I return in a few moments, we can get started."

"Sure thing." Taking the records with a nod, I sit in the seat behind the desk and quickly catch myself up on who we'll be helping tonight.

It looks like so far there is an eight-year-old girl with a suspected foot sprain, an older man with sharp chest pains, a mid-forties woman complaining of a nasty rash all over, and so on. Doesn't appear anybody is bleeding, which is always a good thing.

When Doctor Worthington returns, we start with the older man, who ends up simply having a bad case of heartburn. After that, we head to the room of the eight-year-old, and the doctor stops me right outside the door to speak.

"Mabel is here with her mother. They recently moved into town and are settling in. Both she and her mother say she was playing outside and tripped in a hole they didn't see in their new backyard. All I need to do is examine it and go from there."

He doesn't expect me to reply. He just fills in me even when I read the charts and I give him a nod of understanding, then we head in.

Only when he walks in and I step into the room behind him, I freeze as my eyes take in the people before me.

The little girl on the bed, with her light brown hair, brown eyes, and pale skin reminds me of when I was her age. She beams at Doctor Worthington when he approaches. It's all I can do to drag my eyes away from her to the woman standing beside the bed, gazing down at the child who is obviously her pride and joy.

If he says anything to me, I don't hear it because I'm taking in the woman, who has the same coloring as her daughter, and who's dressed so finely it nearly hurts to look at her. She gleams, reeking of someone with money, from the styling of her hair to her nails being done, to the clothing she wears, and everything in-between.

A woman who speaks to the doctor and doesn't notice the nurse in the room, the one who stands by the door as if she is frozen in time, memories assaulting her from every angle.

God, I can't breathe. It doesn't make sense. When I lift a hand to my chest as if to keep it from pounding straight through my chest, I must make a noise or something because suddenly all eyes are on me.

And that's when I see her face and know my worst nightmare, yet number one dream has come true in the least convenient place possible.

There she is. The woman who gave birth to me, raised me for ten years, then threw me away like I was nothing, all for some drugs. The woman who traded me to a man who would've done some terrible things to me if I hadn't escaped. And I hate her. I hate her for doing what she did, and for being too weak to give up the drugs for me.

But most of all, I hate her for the fact I hadn't been enough reason for her to get sober. And here she stands in front of me, regret written on every inch of her face after her eyes widen in recognition of who I am, and I can't say anything.

Everything that could be said right at this moment wouldn't be appropriate. At least, not in front of Mabel, who is obviously my little sister, my fucking flesh and blood, because I have more respect than that. She doesn't know the mom I experienced, that much is clear. She has the life I might've had if my mom had gotten straight when she still had me in her life, but of course, that hadn't happened. She doesn't deserve to see me rip my mother apart for what she'd done, for the fact she'd given up her rights, and yet here she is looking better than ever.

Happier. Healthier. More beautiful than she'd ever been in my dreams.

And all I can think while tears fill my eyes is...why now? Why, after all this time, is she here in the place I work, having moved into the town I've spent the last thirteen years of my life in, and standing in front of me? Doesn't she know when she gave me up, she gave up any right to be anywhere near me?

The longer she stares at me, apparently holding her breath to see what I will say or do, the sicker I feel. Until Doctor Worthington catches my attention, a look of concern and alarm mixed on his face.

"Yvette? Are you all right?"

I drag my eyes away from my mother and stare into his. Whatever he sees, it's enough to make him take a step toward me with his hand out, and I shake my head as I step back, preparing to flee.

"I…I think I'm gonna be sick."

I've already turned toward the door when he says, "Go. I'll get another nurse in here."

And so I do. I run, just like my heart and mind and body are telling me to, barely making it to the restroom before I throw up what little dinner I had eaten earlier.

chapter four

Doctor Worthington finds me in the employee break room after he's finished with the rest of the patients with the help of Mary, the other nurse on duty. I'm not sure how long I've sat here with my head in my hands, but when he sits down, he places a hand on my shoulder and gives a heavy sigh.

"Want to talk about what just happened?"

"No."

A beat of silence follows with a softly spoken, "You're near to a spitting image of your mother."

My stomach drops as the breath whooshes out of me in one sharp exhalation at his statement. Of course, he guessed; he's always been one of the smartest men I've met and now that I've worked with.

"I suppose you might've written it off as a strong unknown resemblance were it not for my reaction, huh?"

"Correct. I didn't know when I went into the room the first time, but it's crystal clear now exactly who she is, and her face wasn't exactly hard to read either."

"They live here, Simon. They fucking moved here. What kinda fucking shit luck is that?"

Yeah, I say his name. Not saying men's names isn't protecting me from feeling anything, as Doctor Hawkins — no, as Max pointed out with his simple demonstration yesterday. I still feel emotions, deeply at that, which right now has me wishing I could just fucking escape because the pain I thought I moved past years ago has come back with a hard-hitting vengeance.

"I expect she knew you were here, *Yvette*." I haven't looked at him yet, but I hear the smile in his voice. I know it's aimed at me because of his emphasis on my name in recognition of me saying his. "You looked like you'd been punched in the gut; she simply looked like she'd been caught when she wasn't quite ready for it."

"I don't want to see her."

"You don't have to see her if you don't want to. From what I know, I would say she doesn't seem like she deserves it, but that's ultimately up to you."

"That's the first time I've seen her in thirteen years."

"I know."

"I have a little sister."

"I know. She looks a lot like you."

"She's beautiful."

"So are you."

At that, I raise my head, gazing at him as I quirk a brow at him and joke, "Don't let Elizabeth hear you say that."

"She'd say the same." He grins at me as I roll my eyes. "What? It's true. And besides, it's well known in this town that I'm wrapped around Elle and Sam's fingers."

"Ah, little Sam. How old is he now? Nine months?"

"Yep. Almost ten." His eyes twinkle as his smile grows as big as I've ever seen it. "Crawling now, and so fast. I'm afraid when he starts walking and running, I'm fucked."

The love on his face, and in his voice, makes me ache for something I've never had. Even though Liliana and Richard and the whole Pierce family for sure, loved me with everything they had, it never took away the fact my parents hadn't loved me. At least, not truly. Both of my parents chose their addictions over me and seeing my mother again has brought all those feelings to the surface once more.

I won't avoid her; I can't. I want answers, and at the fucking least, my mother owes them to me. And Mabel, my little sister, deserves to know me, just as I deserve to know her. But I'll let my mother come to me because I have no doubt that's what she plans to do anyway.

To Simon, I tap his hand, give a soft laugh, and say, "Thanks for checking on me. I…I think I'm okay now. And I'm sorry I haven't been to see Sam lately. I promise I'll drop by soon."

He shrugs even as the smile stays on his face. "You're welcome. And just give Ellie a call, I'm sure she'll be happy to bring Sam over to see you. But of course, you may come over anytime you like. Now, let's get back to work."

"Yes, please."

So we do.

But in the back of my mind, I'm wondering about my mother and my sister, and what it all means for me now.

SITTING on my couch watching TV the next afternoon, the sound of the doorbell startles me, and I hop up to see who is at my door. A quick peek through the peephole makes it clear Simon has told the most important person in his life what has gone on: Elizabeth.

With a sigh, I open the door and am unable to keep the smile off my face as she holds Sam straight out to me. He smiles and thrusts his arms out, so I take him into mine and step back to let her in.

Our relationship changed the same day she found out she was pregnant, which she'd found out mere weeks after Stefan died. It was the same day she told me I could live in the house I grew up in, and the house Liliana had given to Elizabeth; the same house I wanted for myself. The house I could now live in until Stefan's daughter grows up and decides what she wants to do with it because Elizabeth thinks it's important she have something that connects her to her father.

Mad as I'd been at her before Stefan died, we've both said our apologies and moved on like the adults we are, but it hasn't been easy getting there. And now she comes over from time to time to check on the house and see how I'm doing, yet she also gives me my space more often than not.

I've come to respect her for all she's gone through and finally admitted to myself a while ago that she hadn't meant to hurt Stefan or anyone else. She simply hadn't known how to cope with what happened to her. And I, for one, know exactly what that feels like, especially right now.

Sam giggles and gurgles in my arms as we head into the living room and sit down. She gives a huge sigh of relief, stretches her legs out as she slouches a little and leans back in the chair as she demands, "Talk to me."

"I'm sure you're here because Simon told you all about it."

She winks. "I said talk to me, not tell me all about it, smartass."

Ah. She got me there. I shrug while Sam claps his hand giddily as I smile down at him. "I'm not really sure what to say or think right now. I'm just shocked to see her, to learn I have a sister, and to know she lives here now."

"A pretty reasonable reaction considering the circumstances, although I'm sure you're dying to go off on her."

"I guess I am a little. I just don't understand. I didn't when I was ten and I don't now. And she… she went on to have a whole other life, with a new child and all. It fucking hurts."

"I wish I could say I know what that's like, Yvette, but I don't. I can't imagine it feels very nice though I believe anyone would be angry learning their parents went to have other children after giving them away." She leans forward and waits to catch my eye before saying, "Whatever you decide to do, you have the right to get answers if you want them. And if it were happening to me, I would want to know, even if I decided after to never speak to her again."

I believe her. I know that before Elizabeth came back here, she hadn't actually ever intended to return, and that's how I know she's changed as a person. Because now she will fight for staying where she belongs, whereas before she chose to run and never look back unless she couldn't help it. And I know that's what I will do.

This place is my home, and the woman whose choices led me to this life is here now too. In the part of me that doesn't ignore how unhealthy my view on love and relationships is, I know I'll have to face her if I ever want to deal with my issues of trust. I just hate when it's pointed out to me by anyone else.

"Well," I finally say with a smile. "Like I told Simon last night, thanks for checking up on me. Now, let's talk about something else."

"Like how Sam kept me up all night due to his teething?"

"Aw. Poor baby." I direct this comment to Sam, who mimics my grin with one of his own as he waves his arms in the air wildly. "You'll be glad for those teeth. You'll need them one day to impress people, so make sure you take good care of them."

Elizabeth laughs, and when Sam starts to fuss a second later, I hand him over to her. "Simon told me he's crawling now, like a pro."

"Did he joke about how he's screwed when he starts walking and running because he's an old man?" She takes Sam's hand and holds them in her own as she assists him so he's standing up, his feet touching the ground. "I don't have the heart to tell him that might be sooner rather than later. Sam's gotten real curious about trying to stand here in the last few days."

"Aw, but that's a good thing. He'll be all independent and ready to get a job."

She laughs again and this time, I join her. It feels good to laugh and know no matter how bad things get, I'm never as alone as I feel. I can count on Penny, Simon, Elizabeth, my other siblings, and my dad.

It's just too bad they can't protect me from the pain I know my mother coming back into my life will cause. Denying it is stupid, and I also know while I can delay it all I want, the day will come when I will have to actually talk to her. There's no avoiding it, and in truth, I don't wish to avoid it. I simply don't know if and when I'll be able to handle it, so I guess at this point, it will have to be something I take day by day.

"Anything else going on?"

Her question jerks me out of my thoughts. "Huh?"

"In your life, Yvette. Anything else going on? Perhaps something exciting?"

I stare at her for a second. Does she know? If so, how? It's hard for me to tell if someone in my life knows something, or if they are just guessing. So I get straight to the point by asking, "I dunno. Depends on if you talked to Penny or not."

"I haven't. But now I know she knows something I don't."

With that, I groan and lean back on the couch, tossing an arm over my eyes with a dramatic flair. "Dammit. Fine. One of the doctors I work with likes me, okay?"

"Doctor Hawkins? He's one good-looking man, and smart as hell too, from what I hear."

"How'd you know it was him?"

"He's the only other doctor you actually work with, and Simon's taken."

"Well," I say with a laugh. "Even if he weren't taken, he's a bit old for my tastes."

"As long as a person is age of consent, age is only a number," she replies with a roll of her eyes, helping Sam get on all fours before he takes off crawling across the room. "I mean, there's no accounting for maturity when it comes to age. Older people can act like children, and younger men might be real responsible and mature for their age. You just never know."

"Still, he's almost old enough to be my dad."

She reaches over and slaps me playfully on my arm. "If he had you at fifteen, sure, I'll give you that. Either way, I'm not sure how old Hawkins is."

"I think he's thirty."

"How do you know he likes you? Has he said?"

I fill her in on what happened, and when I get to the part where he kissed the corner of my mouth, Elizabeth squeals and claps her hands together with the same excitement Penny exhibited.

"Oh, Yvette, that's fantastic." She laughs when I grimace. "What? It is. You don't have to guess whether he likes you or not, so if you decide you want to date him, you've got an in."

"I don't know if I do."

"I understand, I really do." Her voice is soft and full of reassurance because I know she thoroughly understands my hesitance, yet her words firm as she continues. "But from a logical standpoint, if you were just a woman who was looking for a man to date and get to know, would he be somebody you chose?"

"I guess so. He seems decent, has a good job, volunteers at a group home he lived in and is crazy enough to like me. I suppose I couldn't ask for much more."

She lifts a brow as if to say, 'well, that's that' but doesn't say anything else about it. Instead, we both watch Sam play with the toys on the floor and spend little more time chatting about her plans for his first birthday party. A little while later she leaves and I get ready to go to work, where I'll see Max for the first time since that day at the group home.

chapter five

"Yvette. Wait."

I stop in my tracks at the sound of Max's voice following our shift. I'm heading to my car to go home and get some rest as it has been a long and busy night, and every inch of my body aches with exhaustion.

When I turn around, he skids to a halt in front of me, and we aren't far apart at all. If he even bends his head a little, I've no doubt our lips will be locked together in an instant. And no doubt he knows I'm staring at his mouth because it curves up into a smile, making me force my gaze away to look in his eyes.

"Hello." Yep, I greet him as if I haven't been in his presence for a whole twelve hours before this moment. Feeling like a fucking moron, I tear my gaze away with a scowl. "What do you want?"

"You." Well, he's blunt, I'll give him that. With a shake of my head, I go to turn around and he grabs my upper arm with his hand, turning me back to him with a soft plea. "Don't walk away, please."

"Look," I say, yanking my arm away with another frown.

"You've been up for who knows how long, and I know I've been up for roughly eighteen hours, and definitely on my feet for twelve of them. I'm tired and I wanna go to bed."

His eyes light on fire as his smile widens, and mine roll with exasperation because I should've known not to mention a bed after his statement. Lifting a finger, I point at his face. "No. I'm going to my bed, in my house, alone. Goodnight."

He snatches my hand in his before I can turn away again, takes a step closer, wraps his free arm around my waist, and tugs my body against his.

Can't say I didn't see that coming because I did. The hand of mine he isn't holding lands on his shoulder, the other still clasped with his in-between our bodies, until he lifts it to his mouth and kisses my knuckles before releasing it.

"Your mouth keeps telling me no, Yvette, but your eyes keep telling me quite a different story. So which is it?"

"My eyes aren't saying anything."

"So you aren't looking at my mouth right now?"

Dammit. I raise my gaze again and deliberately stare beyond his shoulder. "Nope. I got distracted."

"Liar."

"Yes, I am. So you should let me go because evidently I can't be trusted."

He chuckles, the arm about my waist tightening as the other comes up to cover the nape of my neck. "Nice try. I didn't expect this to be easy by any measure, so you're acting just as I expected you would."

"Again, you should let me go."

I know he will if I demand it, so why don't I? Because I'm enjoying this, dammit. I like that he's taking a chance and in a way, enjoy the fact he is able to read me so well even if I'm not admitting I like him to myself right now. Nope, I don't like him, not even a little.

"And you should kiss me."

"No."

"Should I kiss you?"

"No."

"Why not? Would you stop me if I tried?"

God, his persistence makes me smile and I move my eyes back to meet his. "What do you think? We're in the middle of the parking lot at work, you really shouldn't—"

"Who gives a shit?" He mutters an instant before his mouth covers mine, the close-mouthed kiss firm, sweet, and nothing like the peck he gave me the other day. He opens his mouth a little and grabs my lower lip with both of his lips as he chuckles playfully until I realize he wants me to let him deepen the kiss. Parting my wanting yet also reluctant lips, I gasp as he nips with his teeth in approval, and this opens my mouth enough to let him sweep in with his tongue.

My fingers on his shoulders clench, grabbing the fabric of his coat in my fists, as he groans with pure pleasure into my mouth. I don't know what to do because even though I am aware what french-kissing is, I've never done it, so I try to mimic him. Giving his tongue a gentle touch with mine, he must realize I don't know what I'm doing because he takes the lead, moving and swirling his tongue until we're kissing as if we've been making out with each other for ages.

When he ends the kiss by pulling away, we're both panting hard. It takes a few seconds for me to catch my breath enough to comment, "I thought you said you don't kiss someone unless they're your girlfriend?"

"Will you be my girlfriend?"

I should've seen that coming, and when I shake my head hard, he laughs.

"Then," he says, stepping back as he lets me go with a grin. "I guess I just did. It was worth it."

"If you say so." I can tell he doesn't know what to make of me right then, and that makes me happy. I love nothing more than to leave people guessing. With a lift of my hand and a flippant wiggle of my fingers, I say, "I really gotta get some sleep now. Have a nice day."

Again, I walk away, and again he stands there watching me as I get in my car and shut the door.

But this time, he starts walking the moment the door closes, and a little part of me warms at him trying to make sure I'm safe before heading to his vehicle. Not that I know why he likes me, let alone cares, but I won't spend time over thinking it because I'm genuinely exhausted.

So, the moment I get home, I head straight to bed, and the way his mouth felt on mine for that brief moment is what fills my dreams.

LATER IN THE afternoon at the library, I head up the steps to the second floor where the romance area is located. As I walk past the sci-fi and fantasy area, I notice Max standing in one of the aisles.

Of course, he looks up just as I see him, and smiles as I stop walking. "Are you stalking me now?"

"No."

"Oh." He turns back to the shelf, pulling a book off of it,

and then faces me again. "Well, if you want to, I'm okay with that."

"Not really sure you should encourage illegal and improper behavior."

He comes toward me without responding until he's standing right in front of me, almost as close as he'd been this morning. Flicking his eyes down my body before returning them to my face, he holds my gaze with his own. "You look well-rested."

"I am. My bed is quite comfy." I realize we're talking about my bed once more and I want to smack myself in the forehead for my apparent inability to refrain from speaking about it around him. I nod at the book in his hand in an attempt to change the topic, and it works. "What book is that?"

He lifts it up so I can see and says with a straight face, "The Virgin Queen." Then he grabs my hand and places the book in it. "I thought you might enjoy it."

"Did you? Now, why is that?" I clutch the book in my fingers and drop my hand to the side without even reading the blurb on the back because I know exactly why he's giving me a book with such a title.

"History," he begins, lifting a hand and tucking a few stray pieces of hair behind my ear with a gentle gesture that is at odds with the intense look in his eyes. "Well, it's fascinating. Sometimes you wonder what might've happened if you'd done one thing instead of another. Would you end up in the same place anyway because it was your fate, or does every choice really make a difference in the long run?"

His fingers pause on my neck and he keeps them there as if he is waiting for me to say something, so I do. "I don't believe in fate."

"No?" When I shake my head, he drops his hand but

doesn't step back. Instead, he tilts his head to the side a bit and studies me until I feel like fidgeting. "Have you ever caught sight of someone out of nowhere and thought you knew the person, but you couldn't place them?"

I don't know where he's going with this, or what it has to do with the book, but I only wish I was able to forget some people. However, I've always had the uncanny ability to recognize people even years later. "No. I remember everyone."

"Do you?" He leans in, sliding his hand back behind my neck, before lowering his head and covering my lips with his. The motion throws me off balance, yet I don't need to worry about falling over because he wraps his other arm around me. His action pretty much mirrors the kiss from this morning except this time I know what to do. And all too soon he pulls back with a growl of frustration, letting me go gently before stepping back and running his hand through his hair.

He turns around and for a moment I think he is going to walk off without another word, but he doesn't. Instead, he shoves his hands into his pockets and while still facing away says, "When I was sixteen, I'd been at the group home for two years. One night at dinner, another kid asked everybody what their favorite cookie was. A bunch of the kids named off the usual kind one would expect: chocolate chip, or double fudge. Stuff like that. But, not this one girl. She sat right next to me and when I said my favorite was peanut butter, her whole face lit up and for the first time since she arrived a few weeks before, she looked right at me. She said it was her fave, too. I winked at her and told her with my money from the job I'd recently gotten, I kept a package of them above the fridge, hidden in the cupboard, and I'd be happy to share with her."

With a laugh, he whirls around and gives me a rueful smile. "Do you know what happened?"

My stomach flips with anxiety as I remember exactly what he's talking about and whisper, "She stole them."

"And?"

"Crumbled them up and put them all over your bed, mostly under your blankets." With an amused smile of remembrance, I shrug my shoulders and lift a brow at him in question. "You never said anything to me while I was still there. Why?"

"The bigger question is," he says, stepping closer again with the smile back on his face. "How'd you not recognize me? I haven't changed that much."

"I was ten. It was a long time ago, and I can't say it's a time I like to think about." Now I frown. "Come to think of it, why haven't you said anything to me? We've been working together for a while now and before then, well, you've lived here for a few years."

"I didn't know it was you. After all, you left the home three days after you put the cookies all over my bed, and it's not like they tell us where kids go after they're gone."

"Ah. So how did you figure it out?"

"It was the expression on your face when you saw the home again. You kept studying it, and while I might not have changed, you have enough I couldn't be sure. I remembered your name, and while Yvette isn't popular a name, it's not rare either. So, I asked Simon and he confirmed you were the one I was talking about."

"I can't believe it." And in truth, I don't know what to think, especially since now I do recognize him. What are the chances he would work and live in the same area I do after we met thirteen years ago? It's crazy to even consider how such a thing would occur. "I suppose I owe you some cookies."

"Nah, I bake my own now." Capturing my right hand with his left one, he interlaces our fingers while tossing me a grin. "How about having dinner with me instead?"

"Are you going to leave me alone if I don't?"

He stares at me, as if he's trying to figure out what the correct answer might be, and then nods. "I will, but I would also suggest you have dinner with me once. After that, we can be just friends and co-workers if you'd like."

I consider my options, as well as Penny and Elizabeth's thoughts on the matter, and then I think about Stefan. And my feelings for Stefan, and knowing he wouldn't want me to be unhappy; he never would've wanted me to feel the way I do. But it is so hard to feel as if I deserve anything beyond my misery after the way I've behaved.

And here Max stands, waiting for my answer with complete patience, his eyes soft and warm as if he understands the battle going on inside me. I don't know how he would know; maybe he's lost someone he's loved before, but I honestly can't know that. I don't really know much about him at all except the obvious things I've picked up from working with him for so long.

I know all I can do is be honest with him. He witnessed my meltdown in the E.R. the day Stefan died. He knows how upset I'd been; surely he'll understand why I'm not sure I can date anyone, so that's what I open my mouth to say. Only... he beats me to it.

"I know I'm asking a lot," he says in a gentle tone. "I know how you felt about Stefan and I want you to know I don't judge you. You can't control how you feel, and from what I knew of him, he was a good guy. I know your heart was broken, but don't turn me down because of it. Get to know me, spend time with me, and if nothing else, you'll have a friend who has a lot in common with you."

Damn him. "You make it sound so simple."

"And you're making it too complicated. It's just dinner, not a marriage proposal."

Okay, I laugh because he's right. Even with my complicated feelings on the inside, on the outside it is just dinner and getting to know someone. Which, really, should be a simple, enjoyable thing.

"All right," I say, finally returning his smile. "Dinner sounds good."

"Great." He steps back a little and gives me a cheerful grin. "We're both off work tonight, so I'll pick you up at seven?"

"Sure, but only because I've nothing planned and you're the first to ask."

Lifting my hand to his mouth, he kisses the back of it before letting it go. "Enjoy the book and see you then."

Then, without another word, he walks past me and down the steps without a backward glance.

chapter six

DINNER GOES WELL.

Max keeps it simple and casual, meaning we stay in town and go out for burgers and fries, which is perfect for me. I love nothing more than having a good burger and some hot fries with melted cheese on them.

Talk during dinner is laid-back as well. He doesn't think a public area is a place for the deep, private conversations he wants to have with me, and I agree. So, we talk about work, and joke about betting on when the first snow will fall, among other inane topics.

It isn't until we're done where things really get interesting. Having driven to my house, he had parked in my driveway and we'd walked to the local diner to eat. Now, we step outside after he pays the whole bill, even after my objection, and snatches my hand up in his.

As he interlaces our fingers together, I love and hate the fact I don't want him to let go. The contact is nice, the fact he wishes to hold my hand every time we are close to each other is even better, yet I feel guilty. As if I am betraying my own thoughts and feelings for Stefan, even though I know I'm not disloyal or anything in reality. The hard part is convincing my heart how right my brain is when my heart wants what it wants.

Tugging me close to his side, we walk in silence toward my house, and I think he planned to stay silent the whole way, but it isn't long until he does otherwise.

"So, how's our date going compared to others you've had?"

He catches me so completely off guard with the question I give a sharp bark of laughter and stop walking, which has him pausing as well. When his face fills with confusion, I feel mine flush as I admit, "I've never been on a date before so I've nothing to compare this to."

"Ever?" He looks shocked and dumbfounded; disbelieving to the point it would be humorous if I weren't the one on the receiving end of his bewilderment. "But you're almost twenty-four—"

"What's age got to do with it?" Laughing, I shrug and tear my gaze from his all too intense and speculative one now. "Don't look so shocked; you already gathered I'm a virgin if you giving me that book was any indication. Is it so surprising to learn I've never dated because I only ever wanted one particular person?"

When silence greets my response, I look back at him only to see he appears as if he's about to choke on his thoughts, his mouth hanging slightly open. He glances down at our still connected hands and then back up to my face before saying in a soft voice filled with amusement, "Yvette. The book was a joke. I thought you were out of practice with the kissing but… I never thought you were—"

My embarrassment grows into complete mortification,

making me drop my gaze to stare at my feet as I groan. "Oh, god."

"No." He uses his free hand to lift my chin until our eyes meet and he steps as close as he can. "Don't go all awkward on me. I like when something isn't what I expect. Keeps me on my toes." Then, he chuckles and brings his lips close to mine as he whispers, "The book really is good, though. Alternate history, fate, and romance; I'm looking forward to your thoughts on it."

I don't get to respond, to tell him I've not even begun reading it yet because he touches his lips to mine. It's a simple brush, a tentative gesture as he waits to see what I will do, and I'm not sure honestly. Max was the sweet guy who offered a lonely girl his cookies; the man whose bed I'd covered in those crumbled cookies just because I could. Now, he's the doctor I work with on a regular basis, and at this moment, the man who now knows something about me nobody else does.

And, if you don't count the quick, close-mouthed kiss I gave Stefan that one Christmas evening, Max is also my first real kiss. Something he undeniably enjoys doing with me since every time I'm near him now, he puts his lips on me eventually, and when I smile against his mouth at this, he pulls back.

"Something funny?"

I ignore his question and tug my hand from his, closing the front of my coat, clutching the sides close together. "I'm cold."

"This is gonna sound perverted, but I swear it's not. Come home with me; I have something to show you."

If it wasn't for his disclaimer, I might've been less receptive to listening, but instead, I laugh and tilt my head a little while studying him. "Why? What is it?"

He holds out his hand for me to take, palm up, and directly

asks, "Trust me?" When I hesitate, he jokes, "I promise, your virtue is safe with me..."

For now.

We both know the words hang from his statement, and strangely, it doesn't bother me. Although it helps to have a sense of him after working together, a big part of it's the fact he seems to take everything in stride, including me and my issues. So for the moment, I'll see what he has up his sleeve, and honestly, my curiosity gets the best of me.

"Okay," I say after a few moments, placing my hand — and my trust — in his. "Let's go."

"Good choice."

Hell, I really hope so.

As we pull up to his house, I can honestly say it isn't what I expected.

And what I think must show on my face because he acknowledges it with, "Not what you thought it would be, is it?"

Nope. Nope, it's not.

I've seen Simon's house, and maybe I've forgotten to factor in his age and all because he has a beautiful house near town. A house I know will fit Elizabeth, Simon, and four or five children with their own bedrooms. Honestly, a house similar to the one I lived with the Pierce's growing up, which is the same one I live in now.

Max, on the other hand, lives on the outskirts of town, and it appears he lives in a manufactured home. It looks great, though. Even though the darkening sky makes it difficult to see much, I can see it has a small front deck attached and sits on a suitable size of land where he is all alone. My knowledge of this town means I know the closest neighbor is a half mile away. Realizing we are well and truly alone, I laugh as he shuts off the car, and I open my door to get out.

"It's lovely," I say as he gets out as well, and I mean it. "I like it. It suits you, I think."

"Thank you. Let's go inside where it's warm."

He walks to and then up the steps and opens the door, letting me pass through before coming in behind me. After he shuts the door, enclosing us inside, he turns on a light, and that's when I notice it's much bigger on the inside than it looks like it would be from the outside. I'm betting it's the light decor — beige walls from the looks of it, along with light colored carpet — which makes it appear bigger, and I truly do like how homey it feels.

We're standing in what clearly is the living room, with the kitchen to the right, and a hallway to the left. I know it probably leads to the bedrooms, and after slipping out of my shoes at the same time he does, I shrug out of my coat. He takes it out of my hands and not knowing what else to do as he puts it in the closet, I walk over to the couch and sit down.

"Is this what you wanted to show me?" I ask the question while relaxing on the couch, tilting my head a bit to rest it on the back of the sofa, and close my eyes with a sigh.

"Please, make yourself at home," he says with a chuckle, his voice next to me now as he takes a seat. "And as for what I have to show you, well… we should talk first."

Somehow I don't know if I should be amused or worried. But since I'm here…

"Yeah? Okay." Opening my eyes, I turn my head to focus

on him, only to find him a lot closer than I imagined he would be. "Oh, hi."

"I'm not sure we'll get much talking done if every time you look at me, you've got that glint in your eyes."

"I don't know what look you're going on about. It's just how I look all the time." I'm a liar, I know what look he sees, and I'm ignoring it which is what I want him to do. At least, I think I do. I'm not really sure anymore. "Out with it."

He scowls at me but gives away his amusement when his lips curve at the corners, at which point he mutters, "I need to do something first."

Keeping our bodies from touching, he lowers his head just enough to graze my lips with his, and my breath catches even though I sort of expected him to do it. His eyes give away nearly as much as mine do, and I like when he kisses me, and the way it makes my stomach flutter and my heart clench. Taking advantage of the fact I freeze with awareness, he raises a hand and cups my jaw. Caressing the nape of my neck with the tips of his fingers, his touch spurs my mouth to open under his.

We both moan when his tongue invades my mouth and I bring my hands up to rest on his shoulders, but they don't stay there long as he leans his body into mine from the side. I turn toward him while slipping my arms around his neck as his other arm glides up my side and around my back, where he wraps it around my waist and deepens the kiss.

My heart protests the closeness because with my chest against his we are as close as two people can possibly be while fully dressed, but my body practically sings in total agreement with what we're doing. As we sit here making out on his couch, doing nothing but kissing like two teenagers, I wonder what it would be like to have sex with Max. I'm not a fool; I know love and sex don't have to go together. I haven't stayed a virgin because I need to be in love to have sex or anything; I just haven't done it because I loved someone I couldn't get that close with, and he'd been all I desired. And while my heart still struggles, I definitely find myself attracted to Max.

And while I don't have a lot of experience kissing, instinct tells me this is how it's done. His kisses are sweet, smooth, and seductive as he focuses wholly on me, his hands and body radiating with heat and restraint.

When he drags his lips away, I think he curses under his breath while I sigh with regret at the fact he's stopped. He takes his hands away with a marked reluctance and shoves one through his hair. I now know it's a sign he's holding himself back from returning to what he was doing, and after a second he catches my gaze and smiles at me.

"I didn't bring you here to make out with you, I swear." His smile turns into a grimace when he looks down at his watch, and then back up to me. "There's something we need to clear up before… well, before you decide to date me because it's only fair."

He looks so serious I can't resist teasing him. "Are you a virgin, too?"

With a bark of laughter, he shakes his head and takes both of my hands in his, stroking the tip of my fingers as he gets serious for real. "I'm not a virgin. What I wanted to tell you was… someone else lives here with me."

Not one to jump to conclusions, especially because he doesn't seem like the type to do the obvious scenario that jumps into my mind, I merely say, "Okay, and?"

His eyes drop to my hands and for the first time I feel as if he's the more unsure person between the two of us. "I moved here a few years ago, to this place, because I wanted privacy. Nobody comes here unless they're invited, and that isn't many people at all. And that's because a few months before I took the job at the hospital, my father died."

"Oh, Max—"

"That's the first time you've said my name." He looks back up at me as the grin returns to his face. "I like it. Say it again."

"No. You were saying?"

"Yvette."

Compressing my lips, I shake my head before saying with a scowl, "Mm-mm. You can't make me. Keep going."

"I can't. I need to hear you say it again, it's all I can think about."

Rolling my eyes at him and his antics, I try to keep myself from smiling but fail, giving in with a sigh. "Please, Max, finish what you're telling me."

"Now I just want to kiss you again. My name on your lips is hot." When I scowl at him, he laughs and with a shrug of his shoulders says, "Okay, okay. He died, and no, I didn't care. I never knew him, only knew of him, because my mom told me right before she died when I was fifteen. He knew about me but didn't give two shits. I ended up in the home because he didn't want me and there wasn't anybody else to take me in."

"Asshole."

"Yeah, he was." His eyes drop again, and I get the feeling he's nervous even though he seems so calm. "So, I guess he got married to someone else when I was a kid, and a year before he died, his wife passed away due to a heart attack. When his lawyer showed up at my door, I was pissed. I didn't know the man, and he hadn't wanted me, so why would he leave me every cent he had? It wasn't long until I found out why."

I'm not sure where he's going with this, but this whole topic makes me think of my mother, and that has my heart racing. So I nudge him along to chase away my own thoughts. "And?"

"And turned out he made me guardian of my two half-sisters I didn't know existed."

"Oh. Oh, wow." My surprise has me tugging my hands from his, which makes me feel bad as I see him wince before he looks me in the face again, and then I'm the one to glance away. "Where… where are they right now?"

"Bowling. Charity is seventeen, Ruby is fifteen. They went with one of Charity's friends and her family."

I must be really self-absorbed to have missed the fact he's responsible for two kids. "All this time we've worked together and you realized I didn't know this?"

"You've been pretty deep in your grief and never really had to think about me much before now. I work nights and so do you, while the girls are in school during the day and usually home at night. Not a big deal that you weren't aware of them."

True, all of it, but doesn't make me feel any less awful for not knowing such a detail. I should've been paying attention and known of their existence at the least.

And the fact they are teenagers… I remember what I was like as a teenager and instantly want to tell him there is no way I can deal with it. In my experience, teenage girls are nightmares — I would know, I used to be one — and I am sure they'll find my intrusion into their life as just that, an unwelcome encroachment.

He must see my thoughts and doubts on my face because he moves back into my personal space and pulls me against him before I can even protest. But he doesn't kiss me even though his lips are right by mine, his forehead resting gently on mine, and our breaths mingle when he speaks.

"I'm telling you because I want you to know everything there is to know about me. I know it's a lot to ask, but don't turn me down because of it. I saw it on your face, Yvette, and there's no need to panic. They're sweet girls who've been through a lot and I know everybody says their kids are angels, but I swear it's true about them." He chuckles and gives my mouth a quick peck before whispering, "You know how difficult it is to find a woman willing to date a single man my age with small children, let alone teenaged ones?"

No, I don't. Yet I don't say that while we sit here staring at each other, all my feelings whirling and mixing in my mind as my heart and stomach twist with confusion. I want to be hard Yvette right now; the one I'd been before Stefan's death had torn her to pieces. But I can't be her, not anymore.

After all, I know what it's like to feel unwanted, and here I sit being held in the arms of a man who had lost one parent and been rejected by the other, only for the father who had rejected him to turn around and make him responsible for siblings he knew nothing of. And he had stepped up without hesitation.

I'm pretty sure Max doesn't know of my recent reunion with my mother, if you can call it that. Or the fact I have a sister I knew nothing of until recently. The way our situations are so similar scare me more than anything else. He's a man who will understand completely, and still, I want to shy away from it. I'm so screwed up, I hate it, but I feel like this man is too good for me. I've never been good, and I'm not sure I'll ever qualify as good either.

He sits holding me with all his hope in his eyes and I like him enough I can't say no, can't turn him down flat out. Yet I also can't say yes, not with all my reservations, and my muddled feelings. Which means I say the only thing I think is the right thing to say. "I don't know what to say."

"Don't say anything. As long you don't say no, that's good enough for me." Turning his head a little, he presses a soft kiss on my cheek and pulls back until we're no longer touching except for where he holds my hand, his mouth curving up with pure happiness. "We'll go at whatever pace you like, Yvette. I've got all the time in the world."

Even though I have my doubts, I choose to believe him and nod my understanding.

It may not be much to anyone looking in from the outside, but for me, it's a huge step. One I will end up thinking about hard as my mother's arrival finally crashes head-on with my life.

Oh, and the thing he wanted to show me? Turns out he baked me some peanut butter cookies.

I may have been the one to kiss him first then.

chapter seven

TWO DAYS PASS BEFORE MY MOTHER FINALLY LOCATES ME IN A public place—the grocery store. I don't know why she didn't just come to my house, as I have no doubt she knows where I live, but I'm also glad she hasn't. It's my sanctuary and the one place she will never be welcome.

"Yvette."

Her voice comes from behind me where I stand at the deli, and after the woman hands me what I ask for, I turn around ready to say something scathing.

Of course, the words die in my throat at the sight of Mabel standing beside her, smiling brightly at me.

"I remember you," she says with a giggle. "You're the nurse who got sick. Whenever I'm sick mommy makes it all better. Are you all better now?"

"Yes, thank you. Mabel, right?"

Her toothy grin, one that reminds me so much of my own smile at her age, grows even bigger and happier as her eyes shine. "That's me. And this is my mommy." She grabs her hand and goes from smiling at me to staring up at our mother with complete adoration and a little confusion. "How do you know her name, Mommy?"

That one little question makes it clear my mother hasn't told Mabel who I am, and I relax a little. I'm not sure what my mother wants, but there's no need to hurt Mabel unnecessarily.

"Oh, it's a long story, sweetie." Her eyes flick to her cart before going back to Mabel's. "Mommy forgot to get a dozen eggs. Will you go get some for me, please?"

Mabel nods, not even tossing me a glance before heading toward the other side of the store where the eggs are located, and that's when I speak.

"Can't believe you dared show up in my life this way after what you did."

She doesn't even blink at my tone, although the expression on her face is filled with sadness. "I'm sorry if I shocked you. I didn't know you worked at that hospital. It's not how I thought the first time I saw you again would go."

I hate how I barely recognize my own mother's voice, how sweet it is compared to all those years ago, and the way she keeps her tone reasonable and respectful. My hatred for her burns in my chest and I want her to give me a reason to let it all out, but she knows she hadn't done right by me. It's written all over her face, along with the same regret and guilt I saw the other night evident in her eyes.

"Well, I'll make it easy for you," I say in a low voice because we're still standing close to the deli. "I don't want anything to do with you. It's been thirteen years, I've got a new family and apparently, you went and made a new one. So focus on not screwing Mabel up and forget all about me just like you did before."

"I didn't forget about you, baby. I never, ever would've forgotten about you."

"Don't. I'm not your baby. I'm not anything to you anymore." I nod in the direction Mabel took off. "You get a second chance to be a good mother, and it looks like she's quite happy, but you don't get one with me."

When her lower lip wobbles and her eyes grow misty, I don't even question whether I really hurt her feelings. Seeing nothing but her attempting to manipulate me, I grow angrier the more she speaks.

"I knew you'd be mad, Yvette," she says. "But please, give me a chance. There's so much more going on than you know."

"I knew all I needed to understand when I was ten years old, Arlene." My deliberate use of her first name makes her flinch. I feel a small jolt of victory at getting to her, even though it's quickly followed up with regret that I'll never get to know my sister because of how our mother has ruined our relationship. And, of course, how I refuse to let her get away with it now no matter how many tears she cries. "Those memories are enough to last me a lifetime."

"Please," she whispers now, tears sliding down cheeks, which she swipes at with the back of her hand. "Come by the house tomorrow during school hours." She rattles off her address, followed by a deep breath. "Your father and I want to talk—"

"My father?" Horror floods through me at the idea she married my scumbag of a father and I hold up a hand to halt her from speaking again. "I want nothing to do with that fucker."

"No, baby, your real father. I married him. Please, come to the house tomorrow and let me explain."

My mouth drops open as I wonder what the hell she's going on about, but I don't get the chance to respond as Mabel comes walking back up.

She frowns at seeing her mom crying, then turns her eyes to me with a deeper scowl. "Why is mommy crying? What did you say?"

"Oh, nothing honey." With a hand on her daughter's shoulder, my mom smiles down at her when Mabel looks back up at her. "Mommy was just telling Yvette how glad she was that your foot is okay, not even sprained at all. You know I hate when you even come close to hurting yourself."

Ugh. I hate myself even more right then for recognizing she isn't the stupid woman she'd been while raising me. I don't want to like her; I don't want any new pictures of her in my head. I'm not sure I can hold onto my anger if I see she's become a different person, even if it doesn't make up for what she'd done to me.

So I clear my throat and say, "I have to go. Nice to see you're well, Mabel."

Then, before either can say anything else, I turn around and rush away, more confused than ever.

"HOW FUCKING dare you think you can just walk into my life and expect me to forgive you for everything you did!" My voice is raised, my words aimed at Arlene. I refuse to call her my mother at this point.

We're at her house, where she invited me yesterday after telling me she's married to my father for fuck's sake. He stands behind her with a grim look on his face, his hands resting on her shoulders with a tenderness I envy. Only this isn't the man I grew up knowing as my father, yet I see myself in him and it leaves me utterly confused and overwhelmed. It's also the reason I blew up when the first thing she did after my arrival was to ask for my forgiveness because apparently all she's ever done is fucking lie to me.

I didn't have to come, but I chose to. And that's because curiosity got the best of me, especially after she somehow got ahold of my phone number and made a call to me this morning. All my life with so many things unanswered, I just can't ignore the desire to know, even if it hurts like hell.

"Yvette," he says in a soft voice, which contrasts with the look of growing anger on his face. "I know you're angry, but you need to listen, please—"

"Shut up!" I point a finger at her. "I'm talking to her. I don't even know you, so you need to stay the hell out of it."

It's obvious he finds what I say rude, as he opens his mouth to say something, but stops when Arlene casts him a glance over her shoulder.

"It's okay, Jerry," she says in a gentle tone, shrugging off his hands to step closer to me with a frown. "Yvette, yell if you want. I deserve it."

"Stop it! Stop being so fucking reasonable. Do you know what you did to me? Do you know what almost happened when you traded me for some drugs? I was ten." I know my voice has risen to a hysterical level, but I'm filled with rage and contempt and hurt and so many other things I don't give a shit. "Ten! I was two years past Mabel's fucking age and you sold me for drugs! And you think I should forgive you? That man could've raped me, killed me, because of your stupidity!"

She shakes her head, taking another step toward me, and I

don't move. I can't. I want her to touch me and hold me; everything a girl wants her mom to do so she feels loved, while, at the same time, I'm not sure I won't hit her if she does. But she keeps coming and I ball my hands into fists at my side to keep from doing anything stupid. She's the moron here, not me, and I refuse to give in to my urge to hurt her because I'm not like her.

I'm not like her, that's what I keep telling myself, but when she finally gets real close, she kneels in front of me and does the one thing I wouldn't have expected her to do in a million years.

She gets so close we are barely a breath apart, and wraps her arms around my hips, resting her forehead on my stomach as she says as tenderly as possible, "I'm sorry baby. Please, if nothing else, know that I'm so sorry for what I did. I wish every day I could take it back and do right by you."

"You can't." My voice cracks as my fists tighten, refusing to give in to the urge to put my fingers into her hair, whether to comb my hands through it or pull it I can't say for sure.

"I know. I know." She tightens her arms for a moment and I hear her sniffle a time or two before she speaks again, her words wobbly. "Giving you up for good, it killed me, but I hit rock bottom long before then. When the woman came to me and told me she would take care of you if I would just give up my rights so you could be part of her family, I said yes because I didn't deserve you anymore. She said she'd pay for me to get help and start fresh, do things as I should've done when I was younger, although she'd do that for me whether I gave up my rights or not."

This catches me off guard, my hands unclenching while my mouth drops open as I gaze down at the top of her head.

"What?" I finally ask as the initial shock passes. "Liliana came to you?"

"Yes. She said we all needed someone to give us a second chance, and I got lucky they didn't press charges for what I'd done. I guess she had some friends in some high places and she said one day she wanted you to know your mother again, and she didn't wish for it to be with me behind bars. But I wasn't allowed to screw up. If I messed up, I'd pay for what I'd done, so I didn't. I got sober and I've been clean for over twelve years now, baby."

I'm not sure what to say, or think, or do, or even what to feel. I never knew. Liliana never told me she met Arlene, let alone helped her straighten out her life, and it just makes me miss her even more.

But something doesn't make sense. Raising my gaze to the man I now know as Jerry, I can't keep the scowl off my face as I glare at him. "And you? Where were you?"

His eyes flick down to the top of her head before returning to mine. "I had no idea you existed. Your mother and I met in a bar all those years ago when I was separated from my first wife, and it was a one-night stand. I never saw her again, not until twelve years ago. She wasn't on drugs when we met the first time." He says the last words as if they should comfort me, which they don't, nor does his explanation.

Oh, I believe he didn't know about me, but it figures. It just fucking figures that would be the truth over everything else I've ever thought to be true.

"Why—" I start to ask my question, but then realize the answer is staring me in the face, and tears fill my eyes as everything I always wondered hit me all at once. "So that's why the adoption took so long."

He nods. "Liliana had me tracked down and sent your mother to tell me. God, I didn't even know I had a daughter until then, and I wasn't in any position to take you on. Not that Liliana would've let me have you; she said you'd been through enough and you needed a stable family. I didn't sign away my rights lightly, Yvette, but they said you were doing so well…I didn't want to disrupt that, not when…"

"Not when I thought another man was my father." I scoff when he doesn't continue, feeling rage surge through me all over again at the life she had led when I was younger, and the lies she told me. "He wasn't much of a man at all."

"No, he wasn't," Arlene says as she rejoins the conversation. "I accept my responsibility for all I did, but he's the person who got me into drugs. I could've said no, but I didn't. He took me in when you were just a baby and things just went from bad to worse."

"I know. I was there. He was a fucking alcoholic who abused you."

"But he didn't touch you, baby. He wouldn't dare."

At that, I lift my hands and press on her shoulders to indicate I want her to quit touching me. She rises and backs away until she stands by her husband once again, tears gleaming in her eyes.

"Didn't matter in the end, you protecting me, did it? You handed me over to a pig for the drugs I assume that asshole supplied you but obviously wasn't gonna happen when he walked out finally."

"That's enough." Jerry's voice — I can't see calling him my father when I don't even know this fucking man from any man on the street — booms with a slice of his hand in the air. "You've every right to be angry and hurt, but the disrespect needs to stop now. Your mother isn't that person anymore and maybe if she'd told me about the pregnancy things might've been different, but it isn't. She—no, we moved here so we could be close to you and you could get to know your siblings, not so you could speak to your mother like this."

"She," I respond with an angry jab toward her, the fact he says siblings not escaping my notice, but I'm too angry to stand here any longer listening to their excuses. "She isn't my mother anymore, though, is she? And you, you're not my father. You both gave me up; Liliana and Richard are my parents. You're both nothing to me, and no matter your reasons, they don't fucking make up for what she did. Maybe you should've asked me what I wanted before you brought your whole life to a place you're not wanted, and I will thank you both to stay the hell away from me."

Neither of them tries to stop me as I stalk past them and out the door, the tumultuous emotions swirling through me sending me straight into the arms of the one person I know will give me the comfort I so desperately need.

Penny.

chapter eight

TURNS OUT PENNY ISN'T HOME. I'M THINKING ABOUT SENDING her a text, but don't want to interrupt whatever she is doing. Penny's rarely not home, so I know if she's out, she is most likely busy.

I'm not sure where else to go because, in this moment, the only person I want to face is Penny. I've told her about my mom, but not anyone else, except Simon and Elizabeth of course. I don't want to talk to them either right now, though, so I decide to go for some peace and quiet, and head to the library.

The library's the spot to go because since school is in session, hardly anyone goes there during the week in the daytime. And the building, which is pretty old, has a third floor rarely anyone goes up into even though they're allowed. It isn't real big. It has a few bean bag chairs, a lovely view out the window of the lake, is lit well enough for reading without being too bright, and gives lots of solitude when you need it. Like I need it right now.

After entering, I head for the seat closest to the window,

only to stop cold when I discover a sound asleep Max on the lone couch in the room. Looking down at my watch to see it's nearly one p.m., I step closer to him, wondering how long he's been lying there sleeping, and why he wouldn't go home to sleep since I'm pretty sure he worked last night.

Other than at work, where we talk about our work, we haven't spoken about anything personal, nor have we been alone with each other. Everything is kept professional at the hospital, which, of course, is great, and our schedules will no doubt make it difficult for us to spend lots of time together. I'm surprised to admit this slightly bothers me, but only a little. A small part of me wants to give him a chance while the other dominating percentage wants to say no thanks and stay just friends.

I continue to not know what to make of him having two children he takes care of. Okay, they are teenagers, and they are his sisters, but still. He caught me completely by surprise. I figure I would've heard about them before he told me, but then again, I haven't exactly been paying attention.

Well, I am now, and I'm still not sure what to think.

Not wishing to wake him, I quietly take a seat in the chair on the opposite side of where he lies and open my book. Actually, the book Max gave me to read, because I've yet to start it.

And sitting there reading it, I can see why he suggested it.

It's a fantasy story mixed with a what-if. A Queen, who marries the King because he manipulates her, threatens her family, and yet, doesn't have sex with her. He leaves her alone with no company other than her own for years unless they are to make a public appearance.

I suppose it's a bit silly as I get to the magical part where she finds a way to go back and 'do it over' even though she's told it won't stick. She'll come back to her real life, but she'll get to see what she missed because she hadn't made a different, albeit more difficult choice.

I don't get to start that part, though, jolting as Max's sleep-raspy voice says, "Hey."

Marking my page with a bookmark, I lower the book to my lap before slowly turning my head toward him, smiling as our eyes meet. "Hi, mister I-like-to-sleep-in-libraries."

He doesn't even blush; in fact, he does the complete opposite, his mouth widening in a mischievous grin. "This couch is comfy. You should come try it out with me."

"I don't think so," I reply, moving the book to the table beside me before clasping my hands together in my lap as if I'm afraid they will misbehave. "Even if I was interested in such a thing, the library isn't the proper place to snuggle."

"Says who?"

He seems amused by my comment, but I'm more entertained by his question.

"Who? Um, I dunno, pretty much every etiquette lesson I ever had said something like it, I'm sure." I look away as one side of his mouth lifts in a smirk, changing his grin from a mischievous one to one that can only be described as straight out naughty. "Or, you know, the owner of this place. I'm sure they wouldn't approve of such things."

"You're so prim and proper. It's highly charming."

I shake my head as my cheeks flame. "Prim and proper people don't act the way I have in the last few years."

"Both love and grief have a way of making us all do crazy things. It didn't — and still doesn't — make you any less endearing to me."

"You're quite the sweet talker," I say with a huff, returning my face to his and glaring, something that doesn't seem to bother him as his smile widens even more. "It's a shame I've sworn off sugar."

"Have you? That's not what my empty cookie tray suggested the other night."

Busted, but I recover quickly. "Maybe I was simply completely shocked a man could bake, and so well at that."

"An insult and a compliment rolled into one." He whistles as if impressed. "See? Charming."

My lips curve up in unwanted amusement with him. It's a small victory for him, and one he knows he's won, as he extends his arm and holds out a hand for me to take.

"Come on," he entreats like a naughty kid trying to get another to join in. "You won't get in trouble, I promise. And it will make me happy."

"Nope." I lift a hand, pointing at him for emphasis. "I didn't fall for those tricks in high school, and I won't fall for them now. You're probably plotting how to get me banned from this room so you can have it all for yourself."

Chuckling, he swings his legs until he's sitting up and reaches across the space between us to capture my hand. Then, he yanks me out of my chair, and into his lap. Which, of course, never goes as smoothly as in the movies, so when I'm sprawled across his lap in quite an awkward position, he bursts out into full on laughter while readjusting my body. And when our faces are finally inches apart, he smiles at me once more while trapping me in his lap by wrapping his arms around my waist.

"Hi."

I give in with a sigh, my body visibly relaxing even though I know I shouldn't let my guard down. But, he makes it so easy, mostly because I'm aware if I really want him to let me go, he will without hesitation. "Hi."

"Nobody will come up here, you know. Nobody ever does and I'm here every morning."

"I came up here so your point is invalid."

"Oh, I mean besides you. The librarian — who is a distant cousin of mine, strangely — told me you come up here sometimes when you're upset. So," he says while my brows lift in surprise, "what are you upset about today?"

"Would you be offended if I said I didn't want to share with you?"

"A little, but I won't die if you don't tell me. It would just be nice." He grins at me as I shake my head. "What if I guessed?"

"Doesn't mean I'll tell you if you're right or not."

"But what if I am on the first try?"

I become suspicious he already knows what I came up here upset about. After all, this is a small town, and I'm sure by now even though I haven't said anything, everyone knows anyway. So I shrug at him. "Go ahead. I'm betting you already know, which makes me wonder why you asked."

"Perhaps because unlike most people, I would rather get it straight from you, the person I'm interested in dating, rather than assume something is correct."

"I see." I clear my throat and move my gaze to the window to my left before continuing. "My biological mother has moved here, with her new family, including the man who is truly my father. And she thinks I should just forgive her for everything so we can be one big happy family."

Him relaxing beneath me tells me that's exactly what he wants me to tell him, just as I suspected. "And?"

"And what?" My gaze flicks back to his with irritation. "She can't have it. She doesn't deserve it."

After a few moments of silence, he says in a low voice, "Then you'll always be stuck, Yvette."

"Stuck? What do you mean?" His eyes search mine, and I can practically see him trying to find a way to say what he means, so I glare at him. "Just spit it out."

"Fine." He gives a heavy sigh, moving to grab me by the waist, and lifts me from his lap before placing my feet back on the ground. "But I want to step away from you when I say this."

"Ouch. That bad huh?"

He stands up and walks over to the window, facing away from me with his hands in his pockets, and starts speaking. "I don't want to say I've been where you've been, because while my years spent in the system sucked, I didn't end up there because my mother sold me for drugs. I can imagine it's something you would have a hard time getting over."

"Yes."

"I understand. It's hard to see kids in the group home. It's even harder for most of them to know without a doubt they will be there until they age out, and they will have to start their lives with virtually no support." He turns toward me and leans back against the window, crossing his arms over his chest as he stares at me. "But, you were taken in, you were adopted, and you were given a chance many children didn't get. So, why didn't you use it to your advantage?"

I'm confused by where he's going with this, but I respond anyway. "I did. How didn't I? I did well in school, I went to college and graduated, I have a good job—"

"Yes, you did," he cuts in with a soft smile. "But, did you ever get therapy?"

"A little. I didn't like it, though. I went for about a year, and then I just…I dunno, I said I was fine. They believed me."

"But you weren't fine, were you? You were stuck, emotionally, as a ten-year-old whose mother did something terrible, and for all you knew at the time, a father who walked out. And you're still the same little angry girl."

My chest tightens in a way I don't like at all. "I'm not sure what your point is."

"My point," he says while lowering his voice, stepping closer until we almost touch, but not quite. "My point is that you will never grow if you don't forgive her; not even for her sake, but for your own."

"I've grown." I think my protest comes out strong, but it doesn't; it's a mere whisper…as if deep down, I know better. And I do, I know I do, but he doesn't have the right to say this to me. "I've grown a lot."

"Why did you love Stefan? Do you even know?"

Hearing his name from Max's lips feels like a slap, and it pisses me off enough to snap at him. "Maybe because he didn't talk to me like this."

"Maybe he should've. Maybe he should've made you realize you loved him because he was safe; you would never be together, and you knew it. And you let yourself believe you loved him because nothing would ever happen between you two. You wouldn't get your heart broken, you wouldn't even have to risk it. It was always safe with him."

"No!" I want to escape, but my feet are like solid cement, holding me in place even though I don't want it to as tears spring to my eyes. "It wasn't like that."

"Yes, it was," he says softly, his eyes never leaving me even as they fill with a look of sympathy I wish I could smack off his face. "But it didn't protect you, did it? He died, and your heart broke anyway, even though it wasn't romantic heartbreak. It was the loss of one of the few people who never, ever let you down."

"You don't know what you're talking about," I hiss at him, taking a step back as I cross my arms, like I'm trying to ward off his words and the way they make me feel unsettled. "He let me down plenty of times, it didn't make me love him any less."

"He didn't let you down. He simply loved someone, romantically, who wasn't you. He never let you down, personally."

I don't want to hear this. "Why are we talking about him? This is about my fucking mother, and let me tell you, I won't forgive her."

"You need to."

"No, I don't," I say. "And you know why. It's because she basically threw me away! For drugs. I was her daughter and those drugs were more important than me. How can you even suggest she deserves acknowledgment from me, let alone for me to forgive her? I asked her the same damn thing and she just thinks I should just forget? I loved her and she didn't care about me. So give me one fucking good reason instead of trying to talk about something you don't know anything about."

He sighs, sitting down on the couch, folding his hands together before staring up at me. "I'm telling you to do it because yes, she does deserve it. She apologized! Do you know how many people would give their life for someone to apologize for the way they wronged them? How many people wait their whole lives for an 'I'm sorry' that never shows up? You got damned lucky. You ended up in a family that loved you and took you in as their own, gave you their name. Your mother tracked you down when she didn't have to and said sorry. Does it make up for what she did? No. Does that mean you have to let her into your life? No. But it does suggest you should forgive her because it eats you up inside and is holding you back from trusting anyone."

"You mean you!"

He jumps up with an angry growl, making me step back in surprise. "I mean anyone and everyone, and yes, including me. You don't trust anyone as far as you can throw them, and I know it because I was the same way for a long time. I did the same shit you did and I almost screwed up my life because of it. And you know what, I never got my sorry. My father never apologized, and you know what it took before I could forgive him, even though he's no longer alive? Me getting those girls. That's what it took, that's when I realized that if I didn't let go of my anger, I would never, ever be able to love them the way they deserved."

"It's not the same—"

Lifting a hand, he steps forward at the same time he cups my cheek and cuts with me off with a smile. "Yvette, I know that sometimes, not getting what you think you want most in the world is the hardest thing to deal with. Not getting what you need is even worse. I've been working with you for a while now, and I know more about you than anybody should because not much in this town is sacred. But, unlike most, I also know the girl I met in the home, the one who stole my cookies and crumbled them all over my bed. What that girl wanted more than anything was attention." He leans in, murmuring his question near my lips, making them tingle with awareness.

"How many times did you do something outrageous trying to get your mother's attention before you ended up in the home, hon?"

I give him the answer he already knows in a simple soft breath. "Every day."

"Well, you've got her attention now, Yvette. It might be years too late for your head, but your heart…your heart needs it. You'll never be able to give yourself to anyone, in any form, until you deal with the biggest hurt you've ever experienced."

A tear slips down my cheek, and he brushes it away as I whisper, "I hate you."

He presses his lips against mine in a gentle kiss, his smile growing a little wider seconds before he says against my mouth, "No, you don't, but I'll let you pretend that's true if you want me to."

Shaking my head, I take a step back, stuttering as he lets me go with a sigh. "I—I have to go now."

"All right."

That's it. That's all he says, serving it to me with another gentle smile as he slips his hands into his pockets, and I have the urge to slap the genuine sweetness off his face.

Which tells me it's really time to go.

"You're wrong, you know," I say while turning toward the door, speaking in a loud tone so my words were clear. "I did love him. And Stefan would've told me to forgive her. He was that kind of person, and I probably wouldn't have listened to him either."

And with that, I leave, not really sure how the conversation had derailed so quickly.

chapter nine

THE FIRST TIME I MEET MAX'S SISTERS HAPPENS OUT OF nowhere.

Okay, not completely out of nowhere. We live in the same area; I'm shocked it hasn't happened sooner actually. And even though I've worked a lot recently, which means I've seen him pretty often anyway, we haven't gotten to go out since the little tiff we had in that room at the library.

He hasn't said anything about it since either. When we did work together, we would walk out after our shift, with him holding my hand in his until we reached my car. He would give me a kiss goodbye, releasing my hand with a wink, then jog over to his car and get in. And every time that happened so far, I wondered why he hadn't asked me out again, or even called me because his interest in me certainly hasn't waned.

And now, here he stands in the grocery store, with his sisters and a cart full of food five days before Christmas.

I see them before they catch sight of me. I don't even get to contemplate escaping because Charity — whom I recognize from the photos Max showed me that night at his house — lifts her eyes from the cart at the exact same time I take a step back.

"Look, Max, it's your girlfriend."

The words come out in the high, lilting tones which make her teasing obvious, but that doesn't prevent my eyes from widening in shock at her calling me his girlfriend. I'm not his girlfriend. At least, I don't think of myself that way, but did I miss something before? Is the agreement unspoken and I just don't have enough experience to know better?

Max chuckles as he looks at Charity after flicking his gaze toward me, his tone of slight disapproval at her teasing barely covering his amusement. "Charity."

Then, as she blushes and smiles sweetly, Max regards me with a grin of his own. "She's joking. I've never referred to you as my girlfriend."

Ruby, who stands at the end of the cart, joins in with Charity's sudden laughter before blurting, "No, he doesn't. He just gets this look on his face every time he says your name. It's the kind Freddy gets whenever he's talking about that girl he likes, and I have to roll my eyes because—"

"Ugh." Charity holds up a hand, cutting off her sister, and I bite back a smile as Max groans. "Nobody wants to hear about Freddy. He is such a loser."

"You're just jealous—"

"Hardly. I don't want anything to do with boys and you shouldn't either—"

"Why? I don't wanna be like you, Miss Goody Two Shoes—"

"Girls." Max cuts in, his voice sharp and no longer filled with humor, his mouth in a grim line. "Knock it off."

They both fall into silence, glaring at each other, while Max walks around the cart toward me. Once in front of me, he stops and slips his hands into the pockets of his jeans, smiling once more.

He leans in, saying in a hushed voice, "See? Angels."

"Yes, Angels," I respond with a smirk. "Who apparently know who I am, yet they've never met me."

"We've spent some time with Simon and his wife at their house. They asked who everyone in the photo was one time and as soon as I told them about you…"

"Ah, I see." The photo he refers to is one of the last family photos taken before Stefan died. It's something Elizabeth got a copy of because she's always been like family, even if I used to declare how much she isn't. Dragging my eyes away from his intense gaze, I look first at Ruby, then at Charity and say, "It's nice to meet both of you."

They both just smile at me, and I feel the need to get away before they start talking about Max and I having a wedding or something.

Irrational, definitely, but that's how I feel right now.

Giving him a tight smile, I take a step back while saying at the same time, "I should let you get back to shopping for your groceries. I…uh…I need to get going anyway."

"They aren't for us."

That makes me pause in my tracks out of pure curiosity. "Who're they for?"

Ruby is the one who pipes up, speaking with enthusiastic excitement as she clasps her hands in front of her chest. "They're for the group home! Max cooks for them every year on Christmas, and we help too!"

What is this man, a saint?

I swear, if he had a halo over his head, it would shine a little bit brighter at her words at that second. The growing smile on his face tells me he knows exactly what I'm thinking.

"You should join us," his mischievous mouth says, his eyes twinkling because he's aware he's now put me on the spot, especially when Ruby squeals.

"Yes! You should! It's so great, and you're a nurse right? You like to help people, and these are kids. They are so nice—"

"Gosh, Ruby, stop talking already and let her answer." Charity rolls her eyes at her sister and then looks at me with a smirk. "You will, won't you?"

I feel as if she's openly daring me to say no. Manipulative a little even, especially as Max's smile turns into a full-on grin, and he takes my free hand in his with a puppy dog pout. "Yes. You will, won't you?"

Oh, he plays dirty. Hadn't planned on running into me while at the store, but doesn't even blink or think twice at taking advantage of the current situation to get what he wants.

Don't say yes, don't say yes, don't say yes, don't—

"Okay," my traitor of a mouth blurts out as the warmth of his hand heats mine, and blatantly ignoring the chant in my head because I like him. I also want his sisters to like me even if he and I are only ever just friends. Right, that's totally it. "I mean, I will."

"Great," he says as Ruby squeals once more and Charity's brows lift in distinct shock, which makes me wonder what she truly thinks about me.

After all, I have a good idea what she's heard regarding me since she started living here.

"You want to just come to the house around three on Christmas Day?" He squeezes my hand to get my attention and

I jerk my gaze back to his intense one. "We can go together, start prepping and cooking at four, easier that way."

I shrug while tugging my hand out of his. "Sure. Penny's planning stuff for Christmas morning, but otherwise..."

"Good." Leaning in, he presses a kiss to my cheek.

Then, he chuckles while pulling away as Ruby sighs audibly, and Charity mutters, "Gross."

Yep, she's definitely the one who needs to be won over.

Wait, what the hell am I thinking?

Stepping back at that, I lift a hand in a small wave and say, "See you later, Max. Charity. Ruby."

Only upon exiting the store do I let out my breath and enjoy the way Max had looked at me the whole time — with pure, utter happiness written all over his face.

PENNY CALLS me up to say she needs help setting up for Christmas morning, so I head over the night before.

Of course, she mostly wants to talk about me, and Max, and how I ended up deciding to join him and his sisters on Christmas Day as we get stuff done. So I tell her. She laughs a bit at my retelling of the whole thing, including his sister's bantering, and we end up going to bed pretty late once all the presents are wrapped.

Now, it's the next morning, and I'm sitting on the couch as the doorbell begins to ring while my siblings arrive one-by-one. Adrian and Jerome are the first to arrive, arriving together as always since they share an apartment. These two are often joined at the hip and as far as I know, neither of them are dating anyone.

Adrian plops down beside me after sticking his gifts under the tree, and Jerome sits in the chair to our right after doing the same.

"Hey sis," Adrian says as he throws his arm over my shoulder, pulling me into his side for a hug, and kisses the top of my head. "How are you?"

Stefan had been the oldest, followed by Evan, Penny, Jerome, and then Adrian. I love all of them, but Adrian and I have always been the closest since I came to live with them. At only two years older than me, he'd been the youngest, which meant we spent the most time together.

"Fine," I mumble as he squishes me to his side before letting me go. "You?"

He shrugs as I look at him. "Same as always, I guess." Then he lifts a brow and stares at me. "I hear you're dating some doctor dude."

"Did you? Who's your source?"

"Penny," he replies with a laugh. "She was too excited not to share." He pokes me in my side when I don't say anything. "So?"

"So what?"

"Are you with this...what's his name...Max, right?"

"If by with you mean I'm his girlfriend, then no."

"Why the hell not?"

As I frown at the irritation in Adrian's voice, Jerome bursts out laughing before saying, "Stop harassing her, Adrian, before we all start questioning why you don't have a girlfriend."

"You're one to talk, man," Adrian retorts, turning his gaze from me to glare at Jerome. "Pretty sure we're both single, and that's because you're a terrible wingman."

"How so? I just stop you from hitting on chicks when you're drunk that you'll regret waking up to in the morning."

A third voice filled with humor joins in — Penny's — as she returns to the room and takes a seat in one of the other chairs. "Maybe it's because you're both a little awkward around women and use terrible pick-up lines."

"How would you know?" Adrian's voice is amused, his mock indignation humorous to me as he sits back on the couch and crosses his arms over his chest. "You mean telling a woman she obviously fell from heaven because she's an angel isn't good?"

"Yeah," Jerome says with a scowl of his own. "I could tell her I think she's got nice tits and ask if I could touch one because I wanna know what a real one feels like. You know, since my blow up doll is out of commission."

Both Penny and I groan as Jerome and Adrian crack up at their mutual immaturity.

"And you guys wonder why I won't tell you who I'm dating," Penny says with a smirk, which only makes both our brothers turn their glares on her.

"Long as he doesn't make you cry, Pen," Jerome declares as he leans forward, resting his elbows on his knees while cradling his chin in his hands. "I'm not afraid to kick some ass. And same goes for you, Yvette. The guy makes you cry…he's history."

"Yeah, 'cuz you're really scary looking Jerome," Penny replies with a laugh while giving him a pointed look, mainly because he's a pretty skinny guy. "I'm pretty sure Max could take you."

"Oh, but your boyfriend can't? Nice to know."

Penny flushes but is saved from responding by the doorbell, which she happily jumps up to go and answer.

"Leave Penny alone," I hiss at both of them, and they just smile as I frown and shake my head. "She'll never let us meet who she is with if you guys keep picking on her about it."

"Yeah, yeah." Adrian waves a dismissive hand. "I don't think she has a boyfriend at all."

"Me either," Jerome agrees with a shake of his head. "Never seen her with anyone; she's probably just making him up."

"You guys are terrible. Penny isn't a liar; she's just a serious and private person and doesn't want to share yet."

"Right. Like how you don't want to share there is a woman walking around town who looks like you, except a bit older?"

"Maybe because I'm trying to act like she doesn't exist?" I put my face in my hands with a heavy sigh, feeling undesired tears rising to my eyes.

"Now look what you've done Adrian."

Sitting back, Adrian pulls me back against his side as he tells Jerome, "Shut up." And then, after wrapping his other arm around me, he says to me, "I just want you to know I'm here for you to talk to about it if you want. I love ya, sis, and it can't be easy to see her here."

"It's not," I tell him with a sniffle while reciprocating his hug by circling his waist with my arms. "I want her to leave. I want them all to leave."

"I ran into them at the grocery store. Her, her husband I guess, this little girl and two little boys. They looked like twins, I think they're like five or some—"

"Stop." I move fast, pushing him away and standing up, covering my ears in what I know is a childish manner even as my heart beats faster at learning I've got three younger siblings for sure. "I don't want to know about them. I don't want to get to know them, ever."

"You don't want to know your siblings?" Adrian's voice is incredulous, rising enough my hands covering my ears mean nothing, and he scowls up at me as I shake my head at him. "That's not cool, Yvette. They didn't do anything to you; it's not their fault she's your mother. You don't have to forgive her, but don't you wanna get to know those kids?"

"She's married to my father, actually." I'm so frustrated I practically growl out the words. "So, it's both of them, and they had more kids — making them full-blooded siblings — and I don't blame them. I blame my parents, and unfortunately, I'm not sure I can fucking separate the two, no."

"Oh." His eyes widen while he stares at me, then he grimaces and looks away. "I don't get it I guess, but I just think you get a chance to know them, and you should take it." He returns his eyes to me then, snatching up my hand and pulling me down beside him. "You're an awesome person, Yvette, and a great sister. They're lucky to have you as one, just like we are and have been since you came here."

"Suck up," Jerome says with a laugh as he stands up. "I'm going to get something to drink."

He exits the room as Adrian wipes a tear off my cheek, saying, "I'm sorry. I didn't mean to upset you. I just want what's best for you."

Of course, he's forgiven. I can't stay mad at him for saying what everyone else is saying; I know I'm the one with the problem. "It's okay. It's…hard, you know? I'm so angry with her, but…"

"But you love her. You always have." He smiles at me.

"Look, I know I don't know where you're coming from…but I don't need to have been where you've been at to know it's probably hard as fucking hell not to love your parents, even when they do terrible things. They're one of the few people in the world who can probably disappoint us over and over again, and all we want is for them to love us and be proud of us. We crave their approval, but you don't need her validation, Yvette."

"I know."

"No, you don't." When I glare at him, he laughs and says, "You think you do sis, but you don't. You turned into a great fucking person without her, and in spite of what she did and didn't do. You've got the power now; you can make her pay forever, and she knows it. It's not you who needs approval. Instead, she needs yours, and without it, she's missing a huge part of her life. Got it?"

My lower lip wobbles even as I nod at him. "It's just…hurts, so bad. Even looking at her, I feel nothing except anger and resentment. I thought another man was my father. So now I look at this man she's married to, and he's this whole person I've got no clue about, and it makes me even more mad. Because she kept him from me too."

"Not cool, not one bit, but you've got him here now. I mean, he didn't know all those years ago, did he?" As I shake my head, Adrian sighs and rests his hand on my back, attempting to comfort me. "Well, then he deserves a chance to get to know you, and you should know him. Don't block him and those kids out because you're angry at her. And we'll always be your family sis, no matter what, but they're your family too. You can't forget that and ignoring it won't make it less true."

I don't get a chance to say anything else as both Jerome and

Penny return, and following Penny into the room is Evan, Grace, and Lyndsey. Seeing them enter the room together makes me wonder if they came here with each other, although last I knew they had stopped seeing each other after Stefan died. Or, at least, that's what Evan told me.

Of course I've seen all three of them many times since his death, but we've never spoken about the way I yelled at them in the hospital waiting room. I'd been so upset, so angry, that I'd blamed them both for his death when in reality, they hadn't done anything wrong. They hadn't even been kissing like I thought they had been, even though I ended up learning they were in fact together. However, with the way I felt about Stefan, I didn't — and still don't — have any right to talk or judge.

Add one more thing I have to apologize for to my list.

As Evan places the gifts they brought under the tree, Grace takes a seat in one of the chairs Penny set up across the room from me and gives me an anxious smile. I nod at her right before Lyndsey squeals, "Aunty Vet! I missed you!"

Turning my gaze on Lyndsey, I return her high-pitched greeting and open my arms so she can run into them. The moment she does, I wrap them around her and exclaim, "Lyndsey! I missed you more!"

She giggles, pulls back with her little toothy grin that reminds me so much of Stefan's, and shakes her head to the point her pigtails swing side-to-side. "Nuh-uh. I missed you more to infinity!"

With an over-exaggerated gasp, I cover my heart with one palm and throw my other arm over my eyes, leaning until I hit the back of the couch. "Oh no, you win! Where did you learn to say that? I can't possibly beat you now!"

"You're silly, Aunty Vet!" She snickers and pulls on the arm that's covering my eyes until I drop it, then smiles at me once more, her eyes shining with happiness. "I brought you a present! I helped mommy wrap it, but she said it will make you really happy because I chose it."

"Yeah?" I look over at Grace, who blushes and tosses me another smile before being distracted by Evan, who begins whispering in her ear. Immediately refocusing on Lyndsey, I sit up and lean in close to whisper, "What is it? Tell me. I can keep a secret."

Her eyes round as she shakes her head again vehemently. "I can't tell you when it's your gift!"

"Oh, I suppose you're right." I'm just teasing her, and I give her a wink as she backs up. "You leaving me now?"

"No." She turns to Grace and says in a loud voice, "Mommy! I want to give Aunty Vet her present right now! Can I, can I?"

Grace's whole face softens as she gives her daughter all of her attention and nods. "Of course you may, honey. It's your present, she can have it whenever you want."

Lyndsey claps giddily, turns to flash me another huge smile, and then skips over to the tree to sort through the presents Evan placed under it. After a few seconds, she runs back over to me with the gift and holds it out in both hands palms up saying, "Here you go, Aunty Vet!"

Gently taking it from her, I can't help but smile at the fact it's clear she wrapped the gift and turn it over. Tearing away the paper, I notice it's the back of a picture frame, and turn it over expecting a picture of me and her. Instead, I'm rendered speechless as I stare down at the photo of me and Stefan taken in the backyard of Penny's house the same day he died. He has his arm around my shoulder, and I have mine around his waist, and we're both wearing wide, happy grins.

"It's you and my daddy," Lyndsey whispers, resting her little hand on one of mine that holds the frame as my eyes tear up. "Me and mommy found these in a box of pictures. I told mommy we should give it to you, and she said you probably missed daddy almost as much as I do, so here, 'specially since it's you and him."

"Thank you," I whisper as a tear slides down my cheek. "That was very thoughtful of you."

She nods, throwing her arms around my neck, and as I reciprocate her hug with a warm one of my own, I see Grace swiping at tears rolling down her own face.

When she looks over at us, I smile at her, mouthing a 'thank you' to her as well, which she acknowledges with a curving of her own lips. And her soft expression makes it clear there's no need for me to say sorry because she, too, understands and has already forgiven me.

My single thought as Lyndsey pulls away is that my day can only go up from here.

chapter ten

We're unpacking and prepping the food to begin cooking dinner at the group home when Max looks at the girls and says, "You girls know what to do. I need a few moments alone with Yvette so we can talk about a few things, all right?"

They nod, yet don't get a chance to say anything else as Max takes my hand and drags me out of the kitchen then down a hall into a room, and shuts the door. Instantly enclosed in darkness, I expect him to turn on a light, but it's obvious that isn't his intention when my back is against the door and his body is touching mine everywhere.

Finding it hard to keep a tremor of nervousness from my voice, I manage to quietly whisper, "Max."

"I love when you say my name Yvette," he mutters right before he crashes his lips into mine.

I don't like to use the word crash because it's always seemed so strange to me when people say that regarding kissing, but that's what it feels like he does to me. His lips on mine are fast, urgent and passionate. My brain rushes to catch up with this side of Max, because he's always seemed so in control before when it comes to kissing me, and right now it's like he can't help himself.

At a little pressure of his mouth on mine, my focus moves from my thoughts to what we're doing, and I open my mouth to let him inside while wrapping my arms around his neck. He recognizes this as the blatant invitation it is, mirroring my action by wrapping his left arm around my waist. Pulling my body flush to his, he slides his right hand up my back to rest palm down between my shoulder blades.

Feeling surrounded in his arms is such a strange sensation. The fact every time we kiss seems better than the last makes me want to get closer to him at the same time I wish to run away at the same time. I'm not sure how to react to wanting someone enough I can't stay away from them even though I tell myself I should.

He keeps me in his grip, his hold firm and steady as our mouths mingle and our tongues tangle. My hands slowly creep into his hair as they search for something to stabilize my world at this moment, my whole body responding to his touch, to his kiss. And the desire to have him touch me elsewhere slowly builds throughout every inch of me.

But he doesn't touch me elsewhere. He's a perfect gentleman, as he has been since the moment we met, and when he drags his mouth away with marked reluctance, I'm truly disappointed.

However much I wish he would continue, I sigh and force myself to ask, "What did you want to talk about?"

With a peck of his lips on mine and a tightening of his arms around me, he says, "I want you to say you'll be mine."

"I thought today was Christmas, not Valentine's Day." Yes, I'm deflecting with humor, my heart speeding up at his words.

"Funny." I feel the smile on his mouth as it reconnects with mine and he gives me a firm, sweet kiss on my lips before saying against them, "Be my girlfriend, Yvette."

Half of me wants to agree, the other half… "I don't want to hurt you, Max."

"And I don't want to hurt you."

"I don't know how to be a girlfriend."

I can feel the smile on his lips turns into a full-fledged grin. "All the more reason to be mine, because the best way to learn is through experience."

"What if I mess up?"

"What if you don't?" When I close my eyes with a sigh, it's not long before I feel his hand move from my back and cup my cheek, his thumb stroking my cheek as he declares softly, "Unless you've got foresight, Yvette, you're not going to know what will happen in your life. Not now, not ever. I mean what I said before; we'll go as slow as you want. Well, except for this. I want you as my girlfriend and I'll keep asking until you just say yes."

A soft laugh escapes from me. "Really?"

"Yes. Starting now." He puts his mouth on mine, pursing his lips to peck mine, and then whispers, "Will you be my girlfriend?"

"I—"

"Will you be mine, Yvette?"

My lips curve up despite how nervous I feel as his hand moves from my cheek to cup the nape of my neck. "You—"

"Girlfriend?"

"Max—"

Just like that I'm back up against the door, his hand moving up in my hair to grip it, and his hand sliding down to grab my ass as his mouth comes down on mine. I think he's going to continue what he was doing earlier, wondering if the girls will start to get suspicious and come looking for us if we're gone much longer, but he doesn't. He pulls away again, yet not before he squeezes my ass and presses me firmly against his front to make it clear how much he desires me. Part of me wants to tell him I feel the same at this point.

But, because I want to say something other than a simple 'yes' and he won't quit interrupting me, I remove one of my arms from around his neck and cover his mouth with my palm.

His brows rise in surprise, his mouth curving up into a smile against my skin, and he tries to dislodge me by licking it. It doesn't work because I expected him to do that.

"Listen," I say, pausing long enough he nods to let me know he's paying attention before continuing. "I really like you. I wouldn't let you kiss me if I didn't because I don't let just anyone kiss me." His mouth goes into a full grin and I roll my eyes at him. "Yeah, yeah, I know you know that, but you're already closer than a lot of people ever get to me. You know that right?"

"Yes."

His answer is muffled and I press my palm a little firmer against his mouth while shaking my head. "No talking. Just nod."

His chuckle vibrates against my hand, the one he has on my ass giving the cheek a pinch, making me jump a little in surprise.

I scowl at him until he nods like I want him to, then say, "Good. As for my answer, well, I'll say yes if you answer me one question first." I drop my hand when he looks at me while waiting for instructions or for my question and say with a laugh, "Okay, you can talk now."

"What's your question?"

"If I say yes," I say, taking a deep breath and letting it out slowly before blurting out the rest, my face going hot with a blush. "Will you sleep with me?"

He covers his surprise quickly with a bright and mischievous smile. "Eventually."

"No." I clarify when he cocks his head a little to the side and lifts a brow in question. "I'm not a virgin because I'm saving it for some special occasion or for marriage. I've just... never wanted anyone else. And now..."

"I see." He steps back while making sure I'm standing steady and slips his hand into mine. "So, if I say yes I will?"

"Then I'm your girlfriend."

Clasping my hand tight, he brings it up to his mouth and kisses the back of it, and clears his throat. "Deal. And now we should get back to the girls and cooking dinner."

"All right. Lead the way."

Making sure we're both out of the way, he opens the door, and lets go of my hand as he says, "After you."

"Thanks."

We head back and he stops me just before we go in, kissing my lips once more before whispering, "Just so you know, I like you a great deal — in case it wasn't obvious — which means I would've said yes without you being my girlfriend."

"What?"

Without another word he chuckles and winks at me, then takes my hand once more and leads us both into the kitchen so we can get to work.

Once it's time to leave, we get into the car while Ruby chatters our ears off about random things. Charity doesn't wait before texting her friend to let them know they are both on their way to spend the evening.

Max told both girls we were officially together after re-entering the kitchen earlier. Ruby had squealed with excitement, of course, but Charity hadn't reacted much at all. She'd just given us both a smile and gone back to peeling the carrots, and we both jumped in to get things going.

Once we'd served dinner, we sat down to eat with the girls at a table set up just for us, along with the twelve children living in the home as well as the adults who took care of them. It amazed me how everyone ate while talking quietly amongst themselves, and nothing even close to a food fight happened, as I remember happening at least once when I'd lived there. Then after dinner, Peter, Vincent, and Paul had come over to talk to Max. He'd asked them about school, how they were doing at the home, and assured them he'd be here to play basketball with them again after the new year.

And now, his hand covers mine, where it rests after he pulled it across the center just a few moments ago while driving us back to town. Other than the street lights occasionally lighting up the inside, it's dark, and I stare out the window, deep in my thoughts.

Ever since we left the house and I found out the girls were spending the night elsewhere, the fact Max and I will be all alone hasn't left my mind, especially after the conversation we had earlier.

I wonder if he's thinking the same things I am, and if he is planning on having sex with me as I asked him to. Because now that the moment might be upon us, I'm not sure I want to.

Not ever, just not tonight.

I'm thinking about this so much I barely register the girls getting out of the car. Rather, notice just enough to say, 'see you later' to them before they shut the doors, and Max doesn't say much all the way back to his house either. My car is there, and I'm finally pulled from my thoughts when he parks beside my car and shuts off his.

"Yvette?" I turn to look at him right as he opens his door and the lights pop on, illuminating his face, which is filled with worry. "Are you all right? You've been pretty quiet since we left."

"Yeah, sorry," I say, swallowing while trying to tamp down my anxiety, and give him a shaky smile. "I'm just…uh, tired."

He focuses on me, staring me right in the eyes, and either believes me or can't tell how sick I feel. "Okay. It's nine-thirty. Want to come in with me, or would you rather go home?"

I'm not sure how to answer since I want to do both, dammit. "Um…"

"Hey." He grins at me and lifts a hand to my cheek, cupping it before leaning in and kissing my lips softly. "Quit looking at me as if I'm the big bad wolf. Much as I'd love to get you naked, there's no rush. Besides, tonight I'd rather you just spend the night sleeping next to me in bed if that's good with you."

"Yeah." I'm relieved instantly, the anxiety quickly replaced with even more feelings of like for this man, and a slight blush taking over my face at the controlled fire in his eyes. "I'd like that."

"Well, let's go then because it's cold out here."

At my nod, he moves away and exits the car while I turn and get out as well. And not even a minute passes before we're inside the house where it's warm and toasty.

After we take off our shoes and coats, he walks over to the couch to sit and asks, "What do you want to do? We can watch a movie. Or would you rather talk? You didn't say much about your morning with your sister."

Following him, I take a seat beside him and shrug. "Oh. Well, we didn't do much. Opened presents, sat around and talked, had some lunch. Everybody was there, including Elizabeth, Simon, and Samuel. I love that little boy, he's so cute."

"He is," he agrees as he puts his arm around my shoulder and pulls me into his side, where I happily snuggle in while resting a palm flat against his chest. "Did you get anything good?"

"I did. Quite a few things." Not really wanting to bring up Lyndsey's gift nor Stefan for fear it would make me tear up, I ask, "How about you? Did the girls get everything they wanted?"

His laughter rumbles against my ear as he says, "Hardly. However, they're such good kids, they got something they needed and a few things they wanted. I love seeing their faces as they open presents; it's one of the best feelings in the world, especially because they both know how genuinely lucky they are."

"And you?"

"Oh, my present is sitting next to me."

A giggle escapes even as I roll my eyes, another blush stealing over my cheeks. "Flatterer."

"Never. I only speak the truth. Having you agree to be my

girlfriend is all I wanted. I can even show you the letter I wrote to Santa if you want."

We both laugh at that as I shake my head, and after a few minutes where we sit in total companionable silence, I let out a long, slow yawn. Max follows with a loud one of his own, and after removing his arm from around me, he stands up and holds out his hand, which I take while getting to my feet.

Leading the way, he heads into the bedroom while I stop to use the bathroom. Of course, I don't have a toothbrush or anything, so I wash my hands and use my fingers to freshen my breath, and follow the light once I'm in the hallway.

He's standing in front of his dresser going through a drawer and looks up as I enter, his eyes catching mine in the mirror adorning the top.

"Do you want something to sleep in?" He holds up an item in his hands. "A T-shirt perhaps? Although I'm pretty sure it would hang to your knees."

"Uh, no. That's ok." I sweep a hand down my body. "I just usually sleep in a tank and um…you know."

His lips quirk at my apparent inability to say the word 'underwear' and he shrugs while putting the shirt back in the drawer. "All right. Well, I'll be back in a few minutes if you want to get settled in."

"Kay."

He walks toward me, his hand coming up to run along my waist as he passes through the doorway where I'm standing, and then heads down the hall.

I'm pretty sure it's the fastest time I've ever taken off my clothes. Slipping into his bed after turning off the lights, I get under the comforter while wearing nothing but my gray tank and black bikini underwear.

I've never slept in a bed next to a man, and my thoughts turn to what it will be like, and whether or not I'll be able to sleep tonight. Max and I have definitely cuddled a lot, and I also can't wait to see if he's the kind of guy who likes to spoon while sleeping. I feel weird thinking I've read about it and it seems nice, but it's true.

The fact I love the way he wraps his arms around me when we're cuddling tells me it'll probably be just as sweet to lie next to him in his arms.

Okay, I think I'm ready to admit I've got it bad for him, at least physically.

And it seems like forever passes before he returns to the room, chuckling as he says, "I like the lights off too sometimes."

Feeling as if I've done nothing except flush red for most of this evening like I am at what he's just said, I say nothing in reply. After a few moments, I feel the bed dip behind me.

"Just so you know," he whispers as he lies down and scoots close to me. "I'm wearing as much as you are, although it's a T-shirt and boxers. However, it's not what I usually sleep in."

"Oh." My breath catches as he rests his hand on my arm while pressing a kiss to my cheek. "What do you normally…?"

"Nothing at all." His kissing moves from my cheek to my jaw, and then up to my ear where he nips the lobe with his teeth. "Pretty sure I forgot to tell you how beautiful you looked today, so consider that me telling you now. Also, you smell fantastic."

"Th-thank you," I whisper, stumbling over the breathless words as my heartbeat picks up speed. His mouth moves back down my neck until his lips touch the sensitive spot at the crook of my shoulder, making me shiver. "So do you."

He murmurs into my neck, "How sleepy are you?"

"Not much."

"Good, because I'm not sure I can keep my hands and mouth off you right now." He moves until his body is over mine, although not touching me, with his hands palms down by my head as he promises, "No sex, just exploring."

I know I mouth the word 'okay' but I'm not sure it comes out more than an almost invisible whisper. Either way, his lips cover mine so gently a pure sigh of enjoyment flows between us, and I've no idea which one of us it came from. Kisses between us are something we've perfected at this point, and our mouths move together as if they've been doing it forever.

Bringing my arms up, I rest them on his shoulders briefly before sliding them up and around his neck, holding on tight as our kisses become slow, intense, and languid. His weight comes down on me moments before he puts all of it toward his left side. He moves his right hand from beside my head to my left side, where his fingers tease the edge of my tank.

He simply rests his hand there until I get impatient and lift my body a little, indicating I want him to touch me, and he chuckles into my mouth as he slips underneath it. With his hand flat against my skin, I feel the heat emanating off him and warming me as he glides it until he's cupping my breast. We both groan at the contact, my body automatically lifting into his touch, and he kisses me long and hard as he flicks his thumb rapidly over my nipple until it goes taut.

"Perfect," he mutters after he drags his mouth away enough to speak, the words nearly lost in my mouth all the same. "Just absolute perfection."

Then, he's stealing my breath once more, his hand alternating between caressing my breast and sliding underneath me to run his hand along my back. Wanting to touch him, my hands mimic his touch; at least, I move them from around his neck to down and underneath his shirt until my fingers are splayed against his back.

I don't know how long we stay like that, just touching and kissing, but all too soon in my opinion, Max pulls his mouth and hands away before rolling to the side. He takes me with him, and when I'm cradled in his arms with my head on his chest, he breathes heavily for a few moments before speaking.

"Time to stop before it goes any further." His voice is thicker than I've ever heard it and also filled with the amusement I've come to know so well. "I don't want to, though."

It's weird when he says that because I don't want him to either, even though I also don't want it to go any further tonight.

The good thing is, my eyes start to feel heavy, and I say with a yawn, "Yeah."

Not only do I hear his laugh, I feel it, and he wraps his arm tight around me for a second while pressing a kiss against the top of my head. "Night, Yvette."

"Mmm," I say while snuggling as close as possible. "Night."

That's the last thing I remember as his warmth comforts me and I fall asleep wrapped in his arms.

chapter eleven

The next morning Max gets called in to work so after a quick breakfast, he kisses me goodbye and we part ways since he has to be there at nine.

I think about how nice it was to wake up in his arms this morning as I drive to the store to do my weekly grocery shopping. Okay, it had thrown me off at first to wake up in a different bed than my own, but it hadn't lasted long. He made me comfortable, and I realized before we left that if I don't focus on anything other than how he makes me feel, us being together is so effortless and real.

It's not until I'm walking around the store pushing my cart that I realize I haven't heard from my mother at all since the day I went to her house. She definitely hadn't called or texted me yesterday on Christmas Day, which only makes me feel as if she frankly doesn't care, even though I told her not to talk to me.

And hating myself as I shop for fruit because even the way I feel about things is contradictory.

I want my mother to put in an effort, at the same time I

yearn to scorn any attempts she makes at reconciliation, and I know part of it's because I want to hurt her like she hurt me. I want her to feel rejected and unwanted because that's how she made me feel as a child.

In some ways I'm doing the same thing with Max. I agreed to be his girlfriend because a part of me really wants it; the part of me that wishes to have a family someday and someone who loves me unconditionally. Okay, and the part of me that wishes to have sex with someone I'm really attracted to. On the other hand, my heart still aches for its first and so far only love, brought back up a little by the picture given to me by Lyndsey yesterday.

Seeing his face next to mine, both of us so happy, has made me miss him all over again. It made the pain a little less old, definitely a bit more fresh, and I'm not sure what to do about it.

I don't know if I can share it with Max; if he'd be open to hearing about it considering his interest in me. I also know I should ask because if I don't, I'll never know the answer, and he may very well be okay with it.

Yet, I'm just unsure of what to do, how to proceed, and all this uncertainty is making me feel ridiculous.

"Yvette?"

The unexpected sound of my name by a deep voice I'm barely acquainted with has me snapping my head up from where I'm apparently deeply investigating the fruits to discover Jerry smiling at me.

It's weird seeing him here in the store, even though I know it's more weird I haven't run into him before now considering he lives in town.

I almost want to smile, because Max was right. Jerry hadn't known about me, it hadn't been his fault my mother never told him, but I'm still pissed anyway. Because he did learn about me when I was still a pre-teen. And even if he'd given me the life he thought I needed, I still would've liked to have known he was my father over that loser dirtbag.

So I scowl at him, turning to put the fruit in my cart, and when I put my hands on it to start pushing, he speaks again.

"Please don't."

I want to ignore it, but he says it so softly, so sweetly, and with more than a little sadness that makes it so I can't. Turning back to face him, I cross my arms over my chest and say, "Hi."

"I'm all alone." He slips his hands into his pockets, looking uncertain as he stands not even five feet from me, and gives me an uncertain smile this time. "I saw you and well, I was hoping you'd be willing to join me for something to eat."

"Right now?"

He shakes his head. "No. We can do lunch later if you're up for it, or another time. Just let me know when."

"All right." I look down at my cart, then at my watch, and finally back at him. "What about the diner at noon? That work for you?"

Smiling with undeniable relief, he nods and takes a step back. "Sure, I'll see you then."

"Kay."

He turns toward the front of the store and walks away, leaving me to finish up shopping and wonder what having lunch with him will feel like. And also if I can manage to have a relationship with him while not having one with my mother.

Something tells me it won't be that simple — or likely — at all.

When I arrive at the diner five minutes early, Jerry's already there waiting for me.

Score one for him. I love when people are early or right on time; anything else is disrespectful and ticks me off.

He smiles at me as the door shuts behind me, and steps to stand beside me as he asks, "Any preference on where we sit?"

Shaking my head, I walk to the nearest booth and sit down, with him sliding in on the opposite side to face me. Immediately picking up the menu, he peruses it…while I study him.

For a brief moment, I'm amused by how much of myself I see in him, now that I'm bothering to look.

Sure, I am a spitting image of Arlene, with my medium brown hair, dark brown eyes, and pale skin, along with having the same high cheekbones and chin she does. But the rest of me? The rest of me is all him; his hairline, his nose, his eyelashes. Height wise, I think I'm between them at five-six while Arlene is five-three and I'll guess my father is about five-ten. He's got black hair with a little gray throughout it and captivating eyes which look mixed between turquoise and emerald.

I wonder if the boys look like him or her.

I frown at the random thought at the same time he looks up, and his instant scowl mirrors my own as he asks, "What's wrong?"

He seems sincerely concerned, and I did agree to have lunch with him, but the childish part of me doesn't want to act like a grown up right now, and my reply is rude. "Aren't you a little old to have kids so young?"

Instead of getting offended or something, he laughs and shoves a hand through his hair. "It's the gray, isn't it? And even if you consider forty-five old, the answer to your question is no."

"What?" My eyebrows shoot up at that as I remember what he said about him and my mother having a one-night stand. "You were separated from your first wife at twenty-one? When did you freaking get married the first time?"

"I see you've got my rock-solid memory." His amusement is undoubtedly rising and when I scowl at him even more, he clears his throat and shrugs. "We were married at seventeen. Our parents weren't too bright to allow such a thing, but hey, we gave it our best shot."

I make sure my skepticism is apparent as I say, "Right."

"I did," he says as the waitress approaches finally. "And I didn't get married again until your mother came back into my life because I take it seriously."

The waitress introduces herself and asks what she can get for us, we give her our order, and then after she leaves, he continues speaking.

"I was young the first time, and stupid. But she's the one who wanted to divorce, not me, and I loved her so I gave her what she wanted."

"That's a bit ridiculous. If you loved her, why didn't you fight for her?"

He leans forward, hands clasped together, and lifts a brow. "To answer that means I have to share something pretty personal, which you may not want to know."

"Sure I do," I scoff, sitting back in my seat and crossing my arms over my chest, continuing to frown at him. "In my opinion, thinking I had scumbags for a mother and father fucked me up pretty badly. So, I'd like to know about the man who is my actual father if you don't mind."

His mouth tightens at me referring to my mother as a scumbag, but he nods and tells me what I asked to know. "The answer is you can't fight for someone who doesn't wish to be fought for. She hadn't slept with me for a year prior to filing for divorce. Even then I felt completely blindsided because we both had so much going on I just figured sex was low on both of our lists of priorities. Turns out she was seeing someone else she worked with."

"Oh," I say with a grimace. "Ouch."

He shrugs. "I gave her what she wanted, then I moved out and moved on. I finished college, went for and received my Masters, worked my ass off, and then twelve years ago your mother walked back into my life. We've been together ever since."

My hands clench at this, my fingers on each hand digging into my palms, as I make a sound of disgust. "How could you forgive her knowing she had a child you knew nothing about? And after you knew what she'd done to me?"

"It wasn't easy," he admits with a sigh, finally sitting back in his seat again as his fingers stay on the tabletop, fiddling with the corner of the napkin which holds the silverware. He keeps his eyes focused on me. "But when I saw her again, I was drawn to her just like the first time we met. She'd been sober for a year by then, was in counseling, and hated herself for what she'd done. She wasn't allowed to talk to you, though, because Liliana told her to stay away and let you have a healthy, ordinary life. She told your mother she could come around when you were done with college because she didn't want your mother's return to screw up your future. Your mom's wanted nothing else except to apologize to you for a long time now."

I'm unable to resist pointing out the flaw in his final

statement even as his reply makes me wonder what other things Liliana did that nobody ever knew about. “She obviously wasn’t in a rush considering I’ve been done with college for nearly two years now.”

“I figured you’d see it that way,” he says with a heavy sigh. “But rearranging our lives to move here took some time, and while she did want to come visit you, I encouraged her to wait. As bad as it sounds, I had no doubt you’d probably slam the door in her face, and I wanted to spare her the pain at that point. So, if you need to blame someone for that, blame me.”

Our food arrives then, and we fall into mutual silence as we consume our lunch.

I wait until we’re both finished before I softly admit, “You’re right. I wouldn’t have listened to a word she said. But at least I would’ve known she felt bad enough to try even in the face of complete rejection.”

He nods as he sets down his fork, taking a drink of water before saying in a gentle voice, “I know you’re angry with her, and you have every right to be. She did a terrible thing, and you never knew her as anything else except your drug-addicted mother, but she truly is a good person. And she loves you. It's taken her a long time to forgive herself, and even though she’s come a long way from there, she wants — dare I say she needs — for you to forgive her. And to be a part of our lives.”

Tears spring to my eyes even though I don’t want them to. “I’m sure she does, but it’s not easy to just get rid of those memories and all the resentment.”

“Even I know you won’t ever forget, Yvette, but you’re my daughter too. I want to get to know you, which will be difficult if you can’t at least tolerate being around your mother. And I want you and your siblings to know one another.”

"They don't even know who I am, do they?"

"No," he says with a shake of his head while pulling out his wallet. "We both decided if you didn't wish to be in our lives, there was no reason to hurt them with that information. They wouldn't understand." He gives me a sheepish look. "At this point we aren't even sure how to give a kid-friendly explanation to them about you being their sister. The boys are young enough not to care, but Mabel..."

I know what he's saying and nod in agreement. "She's smart. She's also old enough to find out if you're lying to her, so it's probably better to tell her a modified version of the truth."

"Yes. That's the direction I'm leaning as well." He pulls money out and places it on the table before standing up. "Will you at least consider what I've said? We can have dinner sometime or something, just the three of us, and talk."

I stare up at this man who is trying so hard to connect with me and to make up for everything. I know Liliana wouldn't be proud of me if I told him no flat-out. She made sure I had a better life, but she also made sure my mother got the help she needed and told her to come back after I became an adult. Liliana loved me, she never let me doubt it for a second, and it's knowing she would want me to give Arlene a second chance that gives me the courage I need.

"I will," I answer while rising as well. "Just...give me a little time, please?"

"Of course." He puts his hand on my shoulder and gives it a squeeze before pulling away. "I want you to know how proud I am of you, Yvette. You've turned in a beautiful, smart young lady, and I'm sorry I didn't meet you sooner." He takes a white business card out of his wallet and holds it out to me. "I know you have your mother's number, but here's mine. You call me whenever you want, and especially when you're ready."

As I take the card from his hand, he leans in and kisses my cheek, then straightens with a final smile and strides away after saying, "Thanks for having lunch with me."

This leaves me staring down at the card in my hand as a strange feeling squeezes my chest, and I shove it into my purse before turning to exit the diner.

It's only as I'm arriving home that I recognize the feeling as one I've not felt much of in a long time.

Hope.

chapter twelve

I HATE SITTING IN DOCTOR'S OFFICES.

When it comes to being a nurse, I love working with patients, but personally, I don't like having to go to the doctor at all myself. Especially when it's a new one I've never dealt with before.

Genevieve Summerfield is the local OB/GYN. Well, she's the only one who has an office in this town; all the rest who also work at the hospital have them in other locations. This is also the first time I've seen her or any OB/GYN in a personal capacity. Terrible, I know. You're supposed to get checked even if you aren't having sex to check for issues, but I've always been rather shy about this part of my life.

However, now since I've asked Max to have sex with me, I have to do this whether I like it or not.

It's hard not to blush as I sit in the waiting room where I recognize several of the other women. I feel self-conscious even though I know I shouldn't because none of them care that I'm here. There's no stamp on my forehead that declares my intention while I'm here is to get birth control so I can have sex for the first time.

When I'm finally called back and placed in a room, I undress and put on the flimsy gown, then sit perched on the edge of the examination bed with my legs crossed. Taking out my phone as I wait, I see a text message came from Max five minutes ago and open it up.

"*I'm taking my break at work. What are you up to?*"

I bite my lip, considering what to say in reply. Although we talked about having sex, we haven't actually talked about anything specific regarding it, and I'm assuming he thinks I'm already on something. Or maybe he hasn't thought about it at all. Thinking about this makes me frown because this is another reason I'm a sucky girlfriend. Shouldn't I know what to say? It is his business, isn't it, since we'll be having sex? Or is it something people just don't talk about?

Ugh, I feel like an idiot as I think perhaps now isn't the time and reply with a nonchalance I don't feel. "*Nothing much. How're you?*"

His reply is instant. "*Missing you. Working a lot as you know. But I'm off tonight. Got plans?*"

"*No,*" I begin, smiling at him saying he misses me and knowing he means it makes my heart skip a beat. "*I was waiting to hear if this guy I'm seeing has plans. And if they include me.*"

"*I bet they do. Probably something along the lines of his place at seven for dinner tonight and other things. Will you accept?*"

Loving the fact he likes to play as much as I do, I give him a simple, honest answer as there's a knock on the door. "*Yes.*"

Slipping the phone into my purse on the chair next to the bed as the doctor walks in, she smiles at me while shutting the door behind her, and holds out a hand in greeting. "Yvette, I'm Doctor Summerfield."

After we shake hands, she grabs the rolling chair, sticks her laptop on the counter, and starts typing into it while asking me a good amount of medical questions. Some of them I'm pretty sure I answered on the paper, but working with doctors as I do I know she's just making sure everything is correct.

When she's all finished with the questions, she asks, "Do you have a birth control method in mind that you'd prefer?"

I haven't, even though I know everything that's offered, and say with a shake of my head, "I'm not sure. As you see, I've never been on anything."

"Well," she says while washing her hands and putting on gloves to do the exam. "As you know, no matter what you use, you should always have your partner use protection as well. This is your first time; will it be your partner's first time as well?"

"Uh…no."

She moves into position and I quickly realize I don't like this exam at all, my fingers clutching the sides of the bed as hard as they can.

"Relax," she says with a soft laugh as she pauses in her actions. "I personally hate these too, but relaxing is best. Would it help if we talked to take your mind off of it?"

"Um…maybe."

"All right." She starts up again as she says, "I think the pill is the best option. You can always change it out later if you want something else, or decide you want something more long-term. Have you and your partner discussed children?"

"God no," I blurt out, knowing I'm probably over sharing, but the mere thought makes me too nervous to care. Joking, I say, "I think I'd like to see how much I like sex first. I may hate it so much I never want a repeat."

"I know you're kidding," she remarks, chuckling as she finishes up. "But if you have any concerns, please feel free to tell me. I am happy to discuss anything with you if you need it."

Giving her an anxious smile, I sit up and clasp my hands in my lap. "I'm just a little nervous is all."

"Understandable." She takes off her gloves, washes her hands again, and sits down at her computer to type something in before looking over at me again. "Communication with your partner is crucial. So as long as you do that, you'll be fine."

"Thanks." It's then I really look at her hands and notice something I hadn't seen a few weeks ago at the hospital. "Hey, did you get married or something?"

She grins wide and holds up her hand with a quick wiggle. "No, but close. My girlfriend and I got engaged at Christmas."

I don't even blink at this because while I had no idea what gender she dated, and I don't care either. Engagements are good news in general. "Wow. Well, congratulations!"

"Thank you!" She stands up and holds out her hand for me to shake, which I do. "Your pill prescription will be at the front desk. Make sure you use extra protection for the first week no matter what. After that, well, that's between your partner and you. Please call if you have any issues or want to use something else."

"Will do. Thanks!"

"You're welcome." With a final nod and a beaming smile, she picks up her computer and heads out of the room.

As I finished getting dressed, my phone pings with a new text message, and I dig into my purse to find it as I open the door to leave. The message is from Max, of course.

"*Dinner? Fletcher's at 7? Yes?*"

"*Ooh, fancy,*" I type back quickly while approaching the front desk. "*Special occasion?*"

My phone dings as I sign the sheet detailing my visit. After she hands me the prescription, I exit the building and walk toward my car while reading his reply.

"*With you? Always. Pick you up at six then.*"

Kind of liking the fact he assumes I'll be there, I check the time and notice it's only two-thirty. Deciding to fill my prescription, since my intention is to start taking it once my period arrives in a few days.

Once that's done, I head home to take a nap before our date.

THE DECISION of where to go after dinner is made in the car on the way home.

Max reaches across the center and laces his fingers through mine, then asks, "My place or yours?"

I squeeze his hand and laugh at his enthusiasm. "Don't you ever have the girls at home?"

"No," he replies with a chuckle of his own and a shake of his head. "Not during the holidays. They want to spend all the time they can with their friends, and they are such good kids I won't deny them."

"Yeah, I can see that."

"And…?"

Part of me wants to invite him to my place, but the bigger Stefan-loving part of myself doesn't think that's such a good idea. It's my private space, the area only family is invited; the house which would've been Stefan's. Rationally, I know it doesn't matter; I know he would be happy I found someone I feel this way for. He certainly never felt the same as I did, and I know it, but my heart just doesn't care.

So, because I want this, I give him the only answer I can. "I think your place is best."

"My place it is," he shoots back instantly, grasping my hand a bit tighter which makes me feel as if he knows exactly why I haven't invited him to my place.

It's silent for a few minutes, and the closer we get to his house, the more I realize I need to talk to him. Communicate like adults should, without embarrassment.

Too bad, because even though he can't see me, I know my cheeks are burning with it as I tell him, "I um…I went to the doctor's today."

"Why?" His voice is immediately filled with concern that makes my heart squeeze. "Were you sick?"

"No." My throat closes up with anxiety and amusement, making me needing to clear it before saying in a soft voice, "I went to get put on birth control."

A pause, then, "Ah."

That's it. Just 'ah' and although it's dark, I turn my head toward him with a surprised look. "We didn't talk about it and I've never had a reason for it, but…"

"Hey." He lifts my hand to his mouth and kisses the back of it. "I can feel the anxiety rolling off you right now. I'm glad you thought about it because I admit I didn't. Not because I don't care, but because I wanted to make sure I could get you naked first." When I snicker a little at that and relax, he says, "I'm kidding. I've always used condoms. What did you choose?"

"The pill. I start in a few days."

"All right. Do you want to wait until after you've begun it? This is all up to you."

"Uh..." Feeling my cheeks turning red again, I try not to stumble over my words while telling him, "No. I'm days away from my period, and I...I really want this. I trust you."

It's the truth. I know even though it's highly unlikely I'll get pregnant at this point, I also trust he's a man who would step up if I did.

"Good. I do too."

When we get to his house a few minutes later, we head inside, and I take a seat on the couch as he walks into the kitchen asking, "Drink?"

The desire to joke is irresistible. "Got any strong liquor?"

"Sorry, miss," he says with an exaggerated and fake southern drawl. "This is a dry house. I've got water, soda, and some weird smoothie concoction Charity likes that I find more than a little disgusting."

"Hmm, I'll pass then."

I hear him pour something, then shut off the kitchen light, and walk back into the living room with two glasses of water. Handing one to me even as I frown, he says, "I know, but you might need it."

"Max..."

"Come on." He holds out a hand for me to take. "Let's go into the bedroom. Strip down like we did last time, watch some TV, and make out. Whatever happens after, happens, because being anything except relaxed will make it not good for you or me."

I melt a little at how much he cares, and the tenderness in his voice and on his face, taking his hand as I stand up with a nod. He leads us down the hall, where we strip down exactly as he said, and climb into bed.

He lies down flat on his back, and I curl into his side, my hand resting on his chest like it did the other night. Meanwhile, his right arm rests under my neck and his left hand is palm down on my leg that's on top of his. Reaching over, he shuts off the lamp, which leaves us in the dark until he turns the TV on and changes it to a sitcom. I don't really know which one because I rarely watch them, but it's funny.

And even though I know I shouldn't, closing my eyes for just a second seems like a good idea.

Which of course it isn't, because I end up falling asleep. Again.

chapter thirteen

THE ROOM IS DARK WHEN I REAWAKEN A LITTLE LATER.

The TV is off, Max's arms remain wrapped around me, and he's snoring a little — enough to be cute rather than annoying. Laughing softly, I ease myself free from his hold to go to the bathroom.

Leaving the room and walking down the hell, it's unbelievable that I fell asleep instead of having sex with him. I mean, his bed is comfy and lying in his arms is great too, but I must've been more tired than I thought. I've been thinking about having sex with him for a bit, and now I have to wait even longer.

Sighing, I finish up in the bathroom, wash my hands, finger brush my teeth, and head back to the bedroom.

"Hey."

The sudden sound of his voice in the dark startles me as I climb back into the bed, and I jump a little, my hand instantly going to cover my heart. But before I'm able to recover, or say anything back, Max has me on my back and covers my body with his.

"I can't believe you fell asleep on me," he whispers when his mouth is a mere breath from my lips. "Wanna make it up to me now?"

In a voice as low as his, I reply, "It's your fault. You shouldn't be so comfy to lay with."

Pressing his mouth to mine is how he responds to that. I wrap my arms around his shoulders while kissing him back, the slow and sweet quickly turning passionate and urgent between us thanks to the desire which has been building up to this point. His body comes down on mine completely so there's no escape from his grasp. With the perfect alignment of our bodies, I feel how aroused he is as he grinds against where we both want him to be.

He moans as my body surges up into him, and I moan at all the sensations hitting me at once. I know we have to go slow because of my inexperience, but I just…want him.

Yes, I admit it. I want him. No point in denying the obvious.

Because as he's kissing me only one hand keeps his body from completely crushing mine while the other explores. And his hand is all over. My clothing isn't a barrier, as his hand slides from my shoulder, down my arm, jumping down to skim my bare leg, before gliding back up to tease the edge of my panties. When his fingers move inward and eventually slip between my legs, I suck in a breath at the same time my body involuntarily stiffens a bit at the unfamiliar touch.

His hesitance is instant, responsive as he pulls his mouth away from mine. "Yvette?"

"You're fine," I manage to say, my face heating at sharing such an intimate confession. "Not used to anybody but me touching me there."

He chuckles, the sound managing to be incredibly naughty and hot, and I love it. “I see.” His fingers move as my body relaxes, stroking me slow and gentle at first through the fabric, and his tongue darts out to lick my lips playfully. “How ‘bout now?”

“Feels good.”

“Yes, it does.” His hand leaves me, but before I can ask what he’s doing, he sits up and suggests, “Let's take off our clothes. Unless you’d like me to take them off for you.”

Even as I reach down to the edge of my tank, my laughter is soft and happy. “Which is less awkward?”

“Both are great to me. But being skin to skin with you is what I think we both want right now.”

He moves to lie next to me as I pull the shirt over my head, then shimmy out of my underwear, dropping them both beside the bed while being glad for the darkness. Nobody has ever seen me completely naked, and even though I’m about to have sex with Max, I’m not sure I want him to see me naked yet. On the other hand, I want to see him nude, and these two facts make me feel so ridiculous I let out a heavy sigh.

Which, of course, Max notices, covering my body with his once more while asking, “Why the sigh?”

I’m silent for a moment because I realize I want him to know all my thoughts. I wanted this between us, so I need to be open no matter how embarrassed I feel. “I was thinking how I’m glad the lights are off because I’ve never been naked around a man before.”

“We have a lot of time,” he says in a low, gentle tone as he lowers his body until we’re touching everywhere. Instantly, the heat of his body and knowing how close we are to having sex turns me on. “But tonight it just means instead of seeing each other with our eyes, our hands and mouths get to do the exploring."

"Sounds like you've thought about this a lot."

"Yes, I definitely have." He feathers light kisses from the right side of my face, down to my chin, and up the left until he's close to my ear. "Haven't you?"

"Mhm," I admit, sliding my arms up to wrap them around his neck as he starts kissing my neck again. "Your skin is so hot."

Feeling him lift his lower body a little, a tiny nervous giggle escapes when he murmurs against my lips, "Spread your legs a bit."

When I do, one of his hands trails down the side of my body, the tips of his fingers leaving a pleasant tingling in their wake. As he reaches my thigh, he grabs onto it, lifting it before he says, "Wrap this one around me."

I feel like this is something I should've known instinctively, while liking the fact he's instructing me at the same time, and do as he asks. I mean, I'm not totally an idiot, I know how people have sex, but now that I'm actually participating, it seems like all my sense has fled. Being naked and so close to him seems to be turning my brain to mush, especially since we haven't really done anything and I'm immensely aroused.

He doesn't bring his body down close to mine again. Instead, I feel his lower body move, releasing his neck as he leans away from me and quickly discern that he's on his knees between my legs. With one hand clasping the knee of the leg wrapped around his waist, he uses the other to lean in a bit and cup one of my breasts. I'm so turned on already my nipples are taut, begging for attention, which he gives the one with a caress using the pad of his thumb.

Back and forth, my little pants of pleasure turn into whimpers when he moves his face even closer to take the bud in his mouth and sucks on it. He uses his tongue to mimic his previous actions, and as his free hand finds its way down between my legs, his chuckle vibrates against my nipple. My immediate instinct is to lift my body up into his touch, an urge I give into without thought.

A little 'ooh' of surprise mixed with pleasure falls from my lips as his fingers discover the entrance to my body, only to elicit a hiss of pure discomfort as he slips the tip of one inside of me.

However, the tinge of pain dissipates seconds later, his finger inching deeper to help my body accommodate him, and combined with the sensation of his mouth it takes every bit of self-control I have not to beg him to go faster.

My body, however, doesn't have that problem, moving into his touch again, which works perfectly with the curl of his finger as it caresses my g-spot.

The resulting hum of heightened arousal shooting through me makes me gasp out, "Oh god, who knew someone else's touch there would feel so amazing?"

He lifts his head, and although I can't really see his face much, I know his gaze is rife with amusement. "I would assume the entirety of the human race who engage in this behavior on a regular basis."

"Yes, I know, but think about it. Who was the first to speak up and say to someone, 'Hey, I think letting me stick my fingers inside you will probably feel good for you. Wanna try it out?'"

Chuckling, he asks, "Yvette, do you really want to discuss the origins of human sexuality right this second?"

He slips another digit inside me while asking that, evoking another gasp from me as well as a whispered, "No."

"Good," he says while leaning in so his lips hover above mine, close enough I feel his mouth turn up in a smile against my own, and his thumb teasing my clit with little evasive swirls around it. "Do you like this, or is there something else you would like me to do that you enjoy?"

Tightening my arms around his neck, I don't bother answering with words. Instead, I move my hips into his touch once more and capture his mouth with mine, telling him with my body how good he's making me feel.

When his fingers move in the perfect rhythm and way to send my body over the edge, he releases a pleased chuckle into my mouth as I gasp, and removes his fingers from inside me. Adjusting our positions, he replaces his fingers with the tip of his arousal and keeps his mouth against mine as he asks, "Ready?"

"Mm-hmm."

When he begins to enter, the strangeness of it more than the stretching feeling has me tensing up, and he pauses with a murmured, "Relax, sweetheart."

Forcing myself to do as he says, he covers my mouth after I've done it and distracts me with his tongue while giving a thrust that isn't hard but firm enough to go deep inside me.

At my sharp inhalation, mostly from the sensations coursing through me, he goes motionless and unlocks our lips to press one to my cheek. "Let me know when you want me to start moving."

Laughing softly, I move my hands to rest on his shoulders and lift my hips into his, enjoying the way he sucks in his breath and tightens his own body in reaction. He takes that as the permission it is and draws back slow before pushing back in the same way as the first time, mimicking his actions inside my mouth with his tongue after capturing my lips again.

There isn't any more talking after that for a while and there's no question once it ends that this is something I definitely want to do again.

In the morning, things between us feel different.

Nicer, even, than they already have been. I don't often examine my emotions, especially after losing my mom and Stefan, but the way Max makes me feel is similar to the comfort I experience around my family.

And while part of me likes it, another part of me doesn't; one I'm really beginning to dislike.

Waking up next to Max after last night is amazing. We're cuddled close, in the same way we fell asleep together last night, and the last thing I want to do is leave the warmth of his arms and get out of bed.

Especially since tomorrow is New Year's Day, making one thing evident to me — dealing with all the shit holding me back is imperative if I want everything in my life to keep improving.

I haven't been able to let go of Stefan, just like the part of me that hasn't released the anger toward my mother, and I'm sick of how it's influencing my life and the choices I end up making.

I know — and have known — that my feelings about those two people aren't healthy to hold onto. However, it's one thing to have them, and another to get rid of them, even while being aware of how detrimental they are.

A tear slips down my cheek as I think of Stefan. He

would've loved Max, and I know he would be so happy for me if he were still alive. But if it wasn't for Stefan's death, I never would've given Max a chance because of my feelings for the man I knew I would never have.

Hard as my attempt is to prevent myself from sobbing, I can't, and barely manage to bring my hands up to cover my face as all the buried and ignored emotions find their way out through the tears streaming from my eyes.

All these years robbing myself for a man who loved me like the sister I was to him and nothing else, and me telling myself it was more than that because I was afraid. Scared to death of letting someone in, letting someone hold me and touch me, and giving them the power Max now has even though I hadn't wanted him to have it.

When he stirs behind me, his tightening hold around me tells me he's awake even as he doesn't speak a word. He kisses the nape of my neck, caresses my stomach gently with his right hand that rests on it, and holds me securely while the sobbing intensifies.

I'm grateful he doesn't ask if I'm okay, doesn't try to fix whatever's wrong, and lets me know he's here for me while I fall apart in his arms.

Wrapped here in his tender embrace is when it hits me that I'm slowly falling in love with Max, and finally acknowledge the truth of his words that day in the library.

It's time to move on and hope for the best.

And not only forgive the one person in the world who should've protected me, but myself as well.

chapter fourteen

We arrive for the New Year's Eve party at Penny's hand-in-hand later that evening.

My brothers make me proud, though. No jokes or teasing from Jerome or Adrian, both welcoming Max with sincere smiles and hugging me before walking off, leaving me sighing with relief.

Max leans in and presses a light kiss on my cheek before murmuring into my ear, "Awfully quiet in here for a party."

He's teasing me. I told him that Penny's parties were more quiet family things with dinner — and sometimes with gifts depending on the occasion — more than anything else.

Bringing him here's sort of a big deal and I can't blame him for enjoying every minute of it, especially after last night.

Penny walks into the living room right as Max takes a seat on the couch, embracing me before pulling back with a cheerful grin. "You look good, Yivvy."

"Thanks. You too, as always."

"Oh." She blushes and drops her arms with a more

subdued smile, flicking her gaze over to Max. "Glad you're here, but just so you know, if you hurt her, we'll hurt you."

It's the first time I've ever heard Penny threaten someone like our brothers do, and I laugh because she actually catches me off guard with it.

Apparently, it amuses Max too, because he chuckles and grabs my hand, tugging me down beside him as he says to her, "I would deserve it."

Even though she joins in with the laughter, she tosses me a wink before walking off when the doorbell rings, leaving me to deal with Max's affection-filled expression while surrounded by my always curious family.

We hadn't discussed why I cried this morning and I wonder how much he knows even though nothing had been said. The way he looks at me…it thrills me and scares me all at once, making me curious enough to ask him softly, "Aren't you afraid I'll hurt you?"

He brings my hand up to his lips, kisses my knuckles, and answers just as hushed, "Being hurt is always a possibility, but afraid? No. I'd rather spend my energy on making you happy instead of worrying."

How does he always know the right thing to say?

Before I can ask, things taking a twist toward the interesting, with Penny getting our attention by clearing her throat from the doorway.

"Dinner's almost ready," she says when we all turn her way, hands clasped in front of her. "But first, there's someone I know you've all been dying to meet."

Her whole face flushes as she reaches somewhere we can't see, and for a moment, the sight of a woman coming to stand next to Penny confuses me — and by the looks on the rest of my sibling's faces, everyone else feels the same.

The woman is taller than Penny, with long blonde hair hanging down her back, and dressed in dark jeans and a white blouse. The fact I recognize her hits me at the same time she glances around the room with a confident smile, her gaze flicking over all of us briefly before returning to my sister's face.

Penny does the same before focusing her gaze on mine and saying in a sweet, tremulous voice, "This is my fiancée, Genevieve."

If a pin dropped in the room right this second, it would be the only noise made.

My sister has been dating a woman and now they're engaged. Wow.

It only takes me a second to process that, next to the fact she's engaged to the freaking OB-GYN that I saw not even a week ago, and the stunned expressions my three brother's sport make it obvious I'm the least shocked out of all of us.

Well, except for Max apparently, who responds to her announcement first with a grin. "Congratulations, you two."

That seems to spur the others into reactions, all my brothers welcoming Genevieve and her relationship with our sister with open arms, and when Penny turns to me as they draw her girlfriend into conversation, my eyes fill with tears.

"I'm happy for you. Why didn't you tell me?"

"I wasn't ashamed," she assures me with a smile and another blush. "But you know me."

She doesn't have to say it, but as previously pointed out by Adrian and Jerome, she's never brought anyone home. She's private and she always has been, so this is a big step for her. "You wanted to be sure. Nothing wrong with that."

"I am." Glancing over at the others, she snickers. "Think I shocked them?"

"Of course, since they were convinced you were making things up. But now I bet they'll be moaning about how their sister can get a girl while they can't."

Her mouth forms a perfect O as she brings up both her hands to cover it, her shoulders shaking with silent mirth, only to give in and laugh out loud with me.

Then, she walks away to join Genevieve as she speaks with everyone else, and I turn my attention back to Max. "Seems like everyone in my family except my two youngest brothers are getting serious with someone."

"And here I thought you were simply using me for sex."

His smile and the light in his eyes makes it clear he's joking, but after accepting how I feel about him this morning, the need to make sure he's aware of my emotions outweighs any fears about what it means for both of us. Keeping my tone light, I cover his hands with mine, lean in and close my eyes while whispering, "So did I, but it turns out I kinda like you for more than your body."

"Must be thanks to my delicious cookie-making skills."

With a soft chuckle, he leans in to kiss me after I roll my eyes at him, only to pull away after the briefest brush of his lips against mine at Penny announcing dinner, leaving me yearning for more and looking forward to receiving it later.

"Yes, that's fine," Max says into his phone to Charity while holding my hand over the table at the diner where we're having brunch the next morning. "I'll see you both at eight and no later." He pauses, then winks at me as he tells her, "Love you, too."

As he hangs up and sets the phone down on the table, all I can think about is how sweet this man is, in every way. He spent hours with my family and me last night, making all of us smile and laugh, and let me decide when to end the evening.

We left a little bit before midnight, with enough time to get back to his place and into bed, where we rang in the new year while in each other's arms. This time, the soft light of the lamp across the room had given us enough to explore one another, and the sex had been even better than the first time.

I can't stop smiling, leaving me happy and content for the first time in…well, for the first time since Stefan's death, honestly. But it's not all due to him.

Some is from feeling free of the version of Stefan I'd drawn up in my head when I dreamed of a future that would've never happened. It's knowing that if he were here, as my brother, he would approve of Max and how wonderful he is to me.

And my newfound relationship with Max is real. Genuine. Sometimes he looks at me and for a moment, I wonder what he sees in me, but the look in his eyes never changes. Affection and warmth, for me, reaffirmed every time he smiles at me, intertwines my fingers with his, or holds me close to him.

He makes believing we have something lasting so easy that the only time uncertainty tries to get in is when he's not around and my self-acknowledged yet not easily defeat-able fear of abandonment tries to convince me to run away.

When he grins at me, lifting my hand to his mouth to press a kiss against my knuckles before letting go and reaching for his drink, I have a sudden and intense urge to round the table just to be closer to him.

But before I can, he swallows his gulp of orange juice and sets the glass back down as his eyes widen.

I ask, "What?" but he flicks his gaze between mine and whatever has made him react this way without saying a word, leaving me to turn just as two people stop beside our table.

For a few brief seconds, as the scent of a perfume I've only experienced a few times yet have already memorized announces the arrival of Arlene, my resolve to forgive her and move on with my life desperately attempts to hang on in the face of my desire to flee.

Looking up into her face as she stares down at mine with a nervous smile, I have to remind myself she isn't the same woman from all those years ago. She's a woman who got and has remained clean, married a good man, and has young children to take care of — my siblings.

When she softly says, "Happy New Year, Yvette," the small catch in her voice reveals how badly she needs me to reciprocate this tiny pleasantry no matter where we stand in regard to each other.

And forgiving her is for me, not her. But I don't feel like she deserves mercy from me, not in my heart no matter how much I know I need to, and it takes everything in me to nod at her before moving my gaze to Jerry's and responding with an equally soft-spoken, "Same to both of you."

"Yvette—"

"Let's leave them to eat in peace," Jerry says, cutting off Arlene by squeezing her shoulders with his hands, and smiling down at me. "Good to see you."

My eyes remain on him even as Arlene sniffles while he directs her past us and toward the booths in the back, only to discover Max frowning at me when I return my focus to him.

Instantly on the defense, because I know where he stands with this, I pick up my fork and ask, "What?"

"She's trying."

"So am I." Stabbing at my eggs, I lift the fork to my mouth and take a bite, swallowing before elaborating. "I didn't want to return her greeting at all, but I did, so don't look at me like that. I know she's changed. Doesn't mean I can just get over my hurt and anger instantly — all because she said sorry — when her actions shaped my whole life. No matter how I ended up, it doesn't give her a pass on what she did to bring us to this point."

He stares at me for a moment longer before his frown disappears and he clears his throat while picking up his own fork as he says, "My apologies. I'm glad you're working on forgiving her and have no right to tell you how to do it or how long to take."

It would be easy to agree with him, to tell him he doesn't, but I don't want our relationship to work that way. How he makes me feel has me opening up to him in a manner similar to how I would with my family. "Something I know about myself is that we probably won't ever manage to have a mother-daughter type of relationship, but whatever ground we find will be because I want to get to know my siblings and my father. I can't avoid her if I want that, so the best I can promise is that I'll tolerate her, and it has to be good enough."

At that, he smiles again and reaches across the table to take my free hand with his once more. "I would never say your attempts weren't good enough, Yvette."

"But would you think it?"

"No. Never. You're growing and taking chances, which is

what matters. And doing our best is really all anyone can do with the life they're given."

We both fall into silence after that, mostly because I'm wondering if that's true, especially at the sight of my mother casting not-so-subtle glances over Jerry's shoulder in my direction.

The quiet desperation in her face almost convinces me to get up, walk over there, and give her the time with me she unmistakably desires.

However, I can't, because I'm not ready for it. Not yet. And even being able to admit it will eventually happen is a step in the right direction for me.

chapter fifteen

My desire to go at my own pace with my biological mother is nothing more than a wish in the wind, though.

A week later, the house phone rings as I'm preparing for work, and what I don't expect is the sound of Arlene weeping on the other end as I say, "Hello?"

"Yvette." She follows my name by sobbing harder and just as I open my mouth to ask her what the hell is wrong, Jerry's voice comes on the line a second later. "Yvette? Are you there?"

"Yes, I am. What's going on?"

After a heavy exhale, his alarm-filled voice asks, "Have you seen Mabel? Is she there with you?"

"No, why would Mabel be with me?"

"Shit." He pauses, mumbling something I can't quite make out, before speaking to me again. "She overheard us talking about you earlier and flipped out. We told her to go to her room and calm down, we would discuss it later, but she isn't there."

Setting down my keys, I sit down in the chair by the phone

and rub my forehead with two fingers. "What exactly did she overhear?"

"She knows about you being her sister. So we thought maybe she might've headed to your place."

Yeah, that would probably explain her leaving. "I see. And how long has it been?"

"A few hours since she heard." The panic increases with every word he speaks and I feel sorry for him because this definitely isn't how any of us wanted her to find out. "Not sure how long since she left the house."

"I doubt she's gone far." Difficult to act like I'm not worried, too, but keeping a cool head in the face of their worry seems like a good idea. "I'll let you know if I hear from her, but you should call the sheriff just in case. He'll let everyone know to keep an eye out for her."

After assuring me he's already done that, Jerry thanks me before hanging up. Then, once I'm sure Mabel isn't waiting outside or hiding in the house — I don't lock the doors when I'm inside it — I leave a note for her about what to do on my door just in case, and head to work.

By EIGHT PM I've left work early and a lot of people in town are out searching in the dark and pouring rain for the still missing Mabel.

I check my house first and she isn't there, so I grab my umbrella and a flashlight. After locking up, I join another group as they walk by my place. We head toward the lake while calling out her name, and when they turn back toward the town, I head for the woods every kid I've ever known loves to hide out and play in.

Yes, the woods were probably already checked out, but won't hurt to check again. Everyone is beginning to worry she's injured herself or isn't conscious, especially if she hasn't managed to stay warm, and it's hard to remain calm while thinking of all the terrible things that might've happened by now.

The darkness increases with every step I take into the thickness of the trees, bringing up my flashlight to watch my step and look for any movement while calling out to her.

"Mabel! It's Yvette." Another step before stopping to call out again. "Mabel! Are you here, sweetie? Everyone is worried about you. If you can hear me, yell out to me and I'll come to you."

Repeating that while going further into the woods, the old dilapidated structure kids used to pretend was a fort tells me I'm near the center of the woods, and right while pausing to call out again, the distinct sound of sniffling and soft crying reaches my ear from somewhere nearby.

"Mabel, sweetie, is that you?" Silence. Smart girl, probably realizing she doesn't know who is calling out for her and doesn't want to give away her hiding place. "Mabel, it's Yvette. Come out, please. You're not in trouble, but it's too cold to be out here."

No response for what feels like forever, and then, her sweet voice thick with tears and wobbly rings out. "I can't, I'm stuck!"

"Stuck where?"

"It's dark in here," she answers on another sob. "Something fell on my legs and I can't get it off."

For a moment, I debate telling her I'll be right back with

some help, just in case, but have a feeling leaving her alone isn't the best idea. Hopefully, it's nothing too serious. "Okay, sweetie, I'm coming in. Are you close to the door?"

"No. In the back."

I gently open the door and move the flashlight around inside until it lands on Mabel, who brings her arm up to shield her eyes from the light as she huddles near the far wall. Lowering the light while putting down my umbrella just in the doorway, catching sight of what looks like some wood of the building's frame covering her legs is a relief, a feeling that's quickly replaced as I realize the roof looks about ready to cave in.

After a few cautious steps closer, I crouch down and wraps my arms around the pieces on her legs, doing my best to lift up and away without hurting her.

"Don't move," I say after moving them to the side and returning to her side to gently check her legs. "Anything hurt?"

"No." She answers on a wail and surges up from where she sits, wrapping her arms around my neck and bursting into tears.

Mabel's too heavy for me to carry, so I let her cry for a few moments before softly saying, "We should get you home. Your parents are worried sick."

"You mean our parents," she mumbles while pulling back, swiping at her eyes with the back of her hands before rising to her feet. "I heard them. You're my sister."

No point in denying it. "Yes, I am, but it's a long story. And no matter what, it didn't give you the right to run away like this and make everyone search for you."

With a sniffle, she nods. "I didn't mean to. I tried to go home and got lost, then it got dark..."

Standing up as she trails off, I hand her the flashlight and point it at the door. "At least, you're okay, that's the important thing. Let's get back so they can call off the search."

Especially with how the wind is suddenly howling and the rain coming down even harder. We'll both be soaked by the time we make it back, even with the umbrella I've been using.

Mabel walks over to the door and opens it, looking back at me while holding the flashlight at chest level so it lights up her face. "Yvette?"

"Yes?"

"How come you don't spend time with me if we're sisters?"

I hate the pain in her voice because not spending time with her has nothing to do with her, but what's worse is that I can't answer right now because it's better to deflect this until later. Discussing this here might make things worse or even harder to get her to go home. "This really isn't the time to talk about that, Mabel. We need to get back."

"Promise me first." Her whole face crumples as she lowers her voice a little. "Promise me you will now since I know."

How can I deny her that? "I promise. I've got to work some things out, but we'll spend time together, okay?"

She nods and steps into the opening of the doorway, but suddenly, a loud crack of thunder makes us both jump. And before I can move another step, Mabel screams, her terrified shout telling me to watch out the last thing I remember as something crashes through the roof and knocks me to the floor.

I DREAM OF STEFAN.

At least, it must be a dream since he's dead.

Yet, there he sits in the chair next to my bed, smiling at me just like he always did when alive as he says, "Hey."

"Uh, hi. Am I dead?"

"No." He chuckles and leans back in his chair, crossing his arms over his chest. "Just knocked out cold by a roof falling in on you, but don't worry, you'll be all right."

"How do you know?"

He doesn't answer me. Instead, he smiles at me again and says, "That could've been your sister hurt. You found her and saved her life."

"I did what any good person would do."

"Yes, you did. And I always thought of you as a good person, even with all that anger you hid behind on the surface."

Suddenly, I'm crying at how sweet he is even though I know how awful I was and sometimes still am, covering my face while telling him, "I miss you."

"I know."

He isn't real, but his arms around me feel like he's actually here with me, so that's all that matters to me at this moment. I cling to him while crying in his hold, fearful he'll disappear any second.

My tears slowly subside until a sense of peace begins to override the places where it hurts the most, and when he pulls away from me, I look up into his face to find him smiling down at me with such happiness and contentment.

"I'm dreaming," I say while lying back against the pillows. "But this seems so real."

"And what if it is? Would you find it hard to believe things like this can happen? That I'm allowed to come talk to you for a few seconds in a part of your mind nobody understands in every way?"

"It doesn't bother me one way or another. But don't think I'll be telling anyone about this; they'll think what happened to me knocked my sense loose, no doubt."

He laughs and it's such a beautiful sound that my heart squeezes, yet the sensation isn't as painful as I know it would've been right after he died compared to now.

"I can see anything I want." He walks over to the window and stares out of it for a few seconds before turning back to me. "And then, there are moments like this..."

He starts to glow a little and a little buzzing in my head begins, which I try to ignore while asking him softly, "What's it like? After death, that is."

Walking closer, he leans in and kisses the top of my head before stepping back, flickering in front of my eyes as he says with an understanding I could always count on from him. "It's just like life, Yvette...it becomes everything you need it to be and without all the pain. But you've still got quite the life to live, sis, and I know you'll make me proud as you always have."

"Stefan, I—"

The words meant to tell him how much he's always mattered to me die on my lips as he disappears from sight. The buzzing grows louder until I cover my ears and slam my eyes shut, wishing for one more second with the man who taught me what love means even though I hadn't been paying attention to his lesson through my grief.

Instead, life intrudes and drags me back to painful reality.

chapter sixteen

My eyes hurt when I finally open them.

Max is sitting beside the bed watching me with a frown, and he doesn't even smile when he notices I'm awake.

However, some of the worries leave his expression as he stands up, steps close before leaning over the railing to press a gentle kiss on my lips after he whispers, "Hey."

"Hi." He draws away and resumes frowning down at me as I notice he's on duty or at least recently ended his shift thanks to his coat and the stethoscope around his neck. "How long have I been out?"

"A few days."

"Really? Induced?" At his nod, I try to smile only to stop immediately at the pain from the attempt. "Ow. Why does my face hurt?"

"A mass quantity of rapidly coloring bruises along with a split lip, although you lucked out and managed not to break your nose when you face-planted if that makes you feel better."

Yikes. "I would smile and laugh at you referring to it as

face-planting if my chest didn't hurt almost as much as said face. So, I better not do either of those."

His relief is palpable as he relaxes his stance and clasps my hand in his, staring down at me with the affection I've come to count on and desire more than anything else in the world.

"This might not be the best moment to tell you this, Yvette, but even though your injuries aren't life-threatening, the fear of the worst happening and leaving me unable to tell you how much you mean to me has made it difficult to sleep since the moment they brought you here."

And there it is… the moment I've known would come and yet, I'm still surprised it's here.

The thing is, I don't know what to say because I'm not there yet. Not afraid, though, and no desire to push him away because of it. Just… need a bit more time.

So, I say the only thing I can think of, that will say everything I can't even voice right now because he understands me just like Stefan did. "Oh, Max, did you really believe how you feel was ever a secret?"

"No, but never hurts to vocalize it." He grins, lifts my hand to his mouth to kiss the back of it, then lowers it to the bed before letting go while I yawn. "Get some more rest. I'll be back in the morning."

No use in protesting since my eyes seem to close no matter how much I want to keep them open and I'm asleep before he even leaves the room.

MABEL BURSTS into my room alone the next afternoon minutes after a nurse informs me I have guests waiting.

She smiles wide at seeing me sitting up and skids to a stop beside the bed before declaring with marked relief, "You're okay!"

Then, she buries her face in her hands and cries, only to lift her head in the thick of it to blubber through her tears, "I'm sorry! You got hurt all because of me and I swear I'll never do anything like that ever again and—"

"Mabel, stop." My interruption is kind and softly spoken as I hold out a hand for her take. "It's okay honey, and I'm fine. No need to be so hard on yourself."

"Mommy and daddy said the same thing, but I'm not stupid." She swipes at her eyes, wipes her hands on her jeans, and then steps close to the bed to grab my hand with hers. "I ran away and got lost, so it's my fault you were out there and got hurt."

"Maybe you saved me from getting hit by a car instead."

She blinks a few times and then scowls at me. "That don't make me feel better."

With a laugh, I give her hand a gentle squeeze before letting go. "All right. If you need me to forgive you, then I do. And thank you for caring so much that you came to come visit."

"Mommy brought me, but she let me come in here by myself." She takes a seat in the chair, crosses her arms over her chest, and levels me with a knowing look far beyond her years. "I think that's cause you don't like her."

I really want to ask if Arlene said something to hint toward that, but I'll refrain. And Max walking into the room with perfect timing saves me before I say something that might get me in trouble.

He walks over to the bed and kisses me before straightening with a cheesy smile. "How's my favorite patient today?"

My answer is as corny as his question. "Impatient to go home."

"Won't be today." Placing his hand over mine, he turns his head to address Mabel with a more natural grin. "Hey Mabel, how are you feeling?"

"Fine, thanks."

"Good." He flicks his gaze back to me and then lifts a brow at her. "Did you tell Yvette about what you did?"

Mabel blushes as I look between them for clarification. "What she did?"

"Yep." He grabs the stool and pulls it toward the bed before taking a seat. "She used the flashlight to run for help, yelling the whole way. Didn't have to go too far since the people you had grouped up with circled back around to help if you needed it, but she definitely made it easier."

"Wow." I really want to know why the group came back around to look for me, but perhaps being glad they did is all I should focus on while smiling softly at Mabel for braving the dark to get help. "Thank you, sweetie."

Her whole expression brightens as if nobody ever thanks her for anything. And at this moment, her face reminds me of the first time I saw her in that hospital room, seconds before I caught sight of the long-lost mother we share.

Yes. Our mother, who's waiting outside because she knows I don't want her here, yet brought my sister here to see me.

Suddenly, I'm exhausted… and weary of not being able to let go; of potentially ruining that look on my sister's face by telling her she's right about me not liking our mother.

She won't end up like me, because she hasn't and won't go through what I did as a kid, and I don't want her aware of what actually happened either. My sister deserves to grow up thinking her mother is great, and so far from what I've seen, great is precisely what our mother has become.

She's not the same woman and I'm not the same little girl she left behind.

Max was right; I have the power, hold it in my hands even, to give or withhold the forgiveness my mother needs almost as much as I do. Not even for wholly her sake, but that of my siblings…of the people I'll always have a biological bond to for the rest of my life.

And I don't want to destroy it, or taint it, or continue making my mother pay for the mistakes she's trying so hard to atone for.

"Max, will you excuse us, please?"

His brows furrow for a moment before his face clears and he stands up. "Sure."

Crooking my finger as he releases his grip on my hand, he lowers his head toward mine to kiss my lips, after which I move my mouth as he turns his head to whisper into his ear, "And invite my other guest in on your way out, please."

He glances at me with a shocked look before covering it with a quick smile. "Absolutely, beautiful. I'll see you in a bit."

Mabel watches Max leave, turns to me as if to say something, but doesn't get the chance as our mother steps into the doorway with a soft knock on the door.

The moment her eyes land on me where I'm sitting up on the bed, her hands fly up to her mouth and by the time she reaches my side, tears are sliding down her cheeks. She doesn't say anything, and I wonder if she's in shock that I've let her come in, or at the way my face is all bruised up.

But mostly I know the first move is up to me to make, and with Mabel looking at us with such hope on her face it hurts my already aching chest, now is the time for taking the first step toward reconciling with my mother.

I lift my hand up and hold it palm out for her to take. She clasps it tightly with hers and sits down on the stool while crying even harder, and Mabel walks over to place an arm over our mother's shoulder.

That's when I know everything's truly going to be all right between us and for once it's not the scary prospect I've always thought it would be.

"Do you want to move in together?"

Max's question makes me sit up straight in bed and turn to stare down at him with wide eyes. "What?"

He doesn't even blink, just stares at me with a neutral expression contrary to the hope in his gaze. "You heard me."

I have no idea what to say. It's been three weeks since I woke up in the hospital and I'm completely healed from all the minor cuts and bruises. During that time, I've mostly stayed at Max's house, with his sisters keeping me occupied when he was at work.

I could've stayed with Penny and her fiancée, but they were busy joining households along with planning a wedding. I guess now that they were engaged, they didn't want to wait much longer to get married.

Otherwise, the only other option would've been my mother's house, and that wouldn't have been a good idea. However, she calls me every day, although Mabel usually takes the phone after a while to chat about her day and remind me that I promised her we would have dinner once I was all better.

As of yesterday, that time had come, and the day is tomorrow. I will finally get to meet my younger brothers and have dinner with the whole family.

Strange to think it and even more so to say it as I have recently. I have one family, I've gained another, and now Max wants to become one. That is what me moving in would entail, after all.

Attempting to interject a little humor while I work through my thoughts, I say, "Haven't we only been dating for a hot second?"

He sits up with a grin and brings his body over mine, waiting until I'm lying back against the pillows before nodding. "I thought you might see it that way."

"And?"

"And how long we've been dating doesn't matter since I love you, does it?"

He says the words casually, his smile widening when I open my mouth only to shut it again without saying anything because I'm not surprised. His comment about caring for me at the hospital had been the less intense version of his feelings for me. I'm only slightly relieved my lack of a response doesn't bother him when he covers my lips with his with soft, sweet, and slow close-mouthed kisses meant to convey his feelings, which is something he does well and always has.

Ending our lip-lock, his mouth barely leaves mine before he murmurs against them, "I've enjoyed having you here these past few weeks and so have the girls. I don't want you to leave, and I know this might be asking a lot, but only say yes if you want to."

I don't know what to say. Now would be the time to admit my feelings to him, to tell him how the last few weeks of staying with him have cemented what an amazing man he is and shown me how good a life we might have together, and that I would love nothing more than to have it with him. He would take care of me and I know if he ever needed it, I would do the same for him.

However, anxiety over the future makes me ask, "You don't think it's too soon?"

"No." He shrugs, and although his smile dims a bit, the light in his eyes doesn't. "Frankly, I'm ready for more than that, but pushing you is the last thing I want to do."

Oh, my heart picks up at that, and even though I know the answer I ask the obvious question because something inside of me wants to hear him say it. "More?"

"Yes, more. Such as marriage and children. Hopefully, both of those before I'm old like Simon."

"Oooh, you didn't just say that!" Both of us chuckle as I take a deep breath and wrap my arms around his neck. "We wouldn't be dating if you hadn't been a little pushy, so I don't think being pushy is always a bad thing."

"But?"

"There isn't a but. I am stubborn and..." Sucking a breath, I admit the one thing I haven't said out loud to him but am sure he already knows. "Afraid of being hurt. I should've gotten help instead of thinking I didn't need it and maybe things wouldn't have been so difficult for me."

He lifts a brow and merely waits for me to continue as he knows I will.

"I'm not saying yes, but I'm not saying no either. More that everything's happened so fast and after the way I've been my whole life..."

Pressing two fingers to my lips, Max stops me in my tracks

and smiles at me like there's nothing I could say that he can't make me feel better about. "Yvette, when you are ready to say yes, I'll be waiting."

His statement and his understanding make me want to say yes right now because I know he means it.

But, he changes the topic by showing me his feelings rather than stating them again, and this moment becomes one of the happiest of my life with many more to come.

Epilogue

THREE MONTHS LATER…

"There. That's the last of it."

Max sets down the box in front of the closet, strides over to where I'm standing by the door and draws me into his arms for a long, deep kiss that demonstrates his pleasure with this turn of events.

"I'm thrilled you finally said yes," he says after his lips reluctantly away from my mouth with a groan and resting his forehead against mine, his eyes closed. "Even if we'll have to move it all again in a few months. My back might recover by then."

Laughing, I wrap my arms around his waist to hug him tight before stepping back with a smile at the realization we'll have our own house together later this year once we find one we can agree on. "That's what movers are for!"

"Great idea." Shoving a hand through his hair, he glances down at his dirty clothes and grimaces and then looks up at me with a grin of his own. "I'm going to shower before the wedding. Want to join me?"

"We might be late if I do that."

His chuckle is decidedly naughty as he grabs my hand, holding it firmly in his grasp and ignoring my protest while tugging me toward the bathroom. "I'm sure Penny will forgive us considering she knew we were moving the rest of your stuff this morning."

"Maybe…"

I let him drag me along because he's correct. Penny, in her infinite patience and kindness, won't care if we're a little bit late because she's the opposite of a bridezilla. Plus, she told me yesterday the time listed for the wedding is a guideline, not the time because she and Gwen just want everyone to be there before it begins. Of course, the fact the wedding's in her backyard is a plus as well.

Not that I'll take advantage of that too much. However, the moment we're finished undressing, Max pulls me under the hot water with him and shuts the door before making me turn around so he can wash my hair.

When his hands are deep into sudsing up my hair, he softly laughs and moves his mouth close to my ear to say, "With everything going on, I forgot to ask what you thought about that book I gave you to read."

"It was good." Removing his hands from my hair, I take that as my cue to rinse out the soap, only to find him staring at me expectedly when I'm done. Stepping forward, I wrap my arms around his neck and step up on tiptoe to kiss his lips. "The ending was sad, but I loved the story. She saw what might have been, then found something she could live with in reality, even though it wasn't something she could openly acknowledge for the rest of her life. And that King was a bastard."

He nods, his face remaining serious and intent on what I have to say. "And the moral of the story is…?"

"That I won't let you pick me another book if it doesn't have a happy ending, and if we keep talking about this, we'll be late for the wedding!"

Any thought of that getting him to hurry up is quickly pushed aside by him grinning and wrapping his arms around my waist to take advantage of our mutual nudity.

Definitely going to be late now.

PENNY'S WEDDING is beautiful as well as perfect for her — and Gwen, of course.

Both of them head down the aisle in pink blush-colored dresses, holding hands and carrying individual bouquets, surrounded by friends and family on each side of where they walk.

Max and his sisters sit on my left in the front row, his fingers are intertwined with mine and have been since we arrived, while Adrian and Jerome are on my right. Grace, Evan, and Lyndsey sit across the aisle from us, with Elizabeth, Simon, and Samuel seated behind them.

Seeing Penny and Gwen stop at the end of the aisle, stand in front of us, and vow to spend their lives together makes it hard to keep my eyes from tearing up. Even harder to avoid glancing over at Max, who's staring at me rather than watching the ceremony, along with wondering what he's thinking at the same time.

The moment they kiss before drawing away from each other, their faces filled with the same love and affection I see on Max's face every day when he looks at me, my emotions aren't able to be held back any longer.

Although we've grown closer and I've moved in, telling him my feelings about him has been the one thing I haven't managed to do yet. Like everything else between us, he's there for me and nudges me along when necessary, but not when it comes to my emotions. The difference is now I can openly admit they are the most stubborn part of me.

Except today, apparently, because now the tears have started and won't stop despite my efforts otherwise. I barely hold back my sobs as Penny and Gwen stroll past us once the ceremony's ended, pulling my hand free from Max's grasp before standing up and rushing for the safety of the house.

Naturally, it isn't long before Max is standing outside the bathroom door where I'm hiding, leaning against the counter with my head in my hands while crying harder than ever before. When I don't answer at his soft knock, he opens the unlocked door and steals inside, pulling me into a warm, tight embrace.

He holds me until the tears subside and when I can finally look into his face, there's only one thing left to say to the good-looking man whose eyes shine with passion for me all the time.

"I love you, Max." It comes out soft, almost a whisper, yet it fills the tiny space we're occupying, loud to me since they are words I rarely say to anyone. And as he wipes a tear off my cheek with the pad of his thumb, I say it again through the emotion clogging my throat because he deserves to hear me say it over and over. "I love you so much."

"Good," he says, pressing a kiss to my lips as both his hands drops away from my face and out of sight. "Because I love you, too."

Then, in the beat of silence that follows, he grabs my left

hands with his right one and lifts his free one to show me the beautiful diamond ring glinting in his hold.

"I didn't plan to propose in a bathroom, but this has been burning a hole in my pocket, and I don't want to wait a moment longer than necessary after hearing those longed for words from your lips." He takes a step back, lifts my hand to press a kiss on the back of it, and leans in to murmur against my mouth, "Will you marry me, Yvette, and build the wonderful life we can have together alongside me?"

The tears blur my eyes again, except this time they are happy ones, and I laugh softly as I say, "What? No asking me to make you the happiest man on Earth?"

"I'm proposing in a bathroom. No need to be cliché by using the standard line on top of it." Another kiss. "Unless it will get me the answer I'm seeking, of course."

"No need." Shaking my head, I wiggle my fingers in his hold and tell him exactly what he wants to hear, and give myself what I want more than anything in the world — a family and a future with this wonderful man. "Yes, I will marry you, Max."

He slips the ring on my finger, and not for the first time, marks a new beginning in our lives. Something I'm ready to experience with the support of everyone who loves me.

And after we head back outside to join everyone at the reception, Max tugging me close to his side to hold me close is sweet, but the best part is when Charity and Ruby squeal at the sight of the ring on my finger.

Nothing sweeter than a family, by blood or choice… a fact I will never forget nor of how lucky I am to have both for the rest of my life.

THE END

about the author

Hey! I'm Violet Haze. I am autistic & the mother of one cool kid. I've been writing and publishing romantic fiction since late 2013. The majority of my stories are steamy romance and *all* of them are stories of true love. Happy reading!

For information on other books you can read, including links to ALL the vendors, visit my website: www.authorvioletthaze.com

Want to contact me?
Email at: violet@authorviolethaze.com

also by violet haze

If I Had You

To Break a Vow

Sugar Baby Lies

Fragments of Us

Hungry Heart

Loving My Angel

Forever His (In the Dark #1)

Forever Yours (In the Dark #2)

Forever Mine (In the Dark #3)

To Love and Second Chances

The Seduction of Luna

Played: A Billionaire Romance

All the Way: A Dad's Best Friend Novella

Bend the Rules: A Dad's Best Friend Novella

Call the Shots: A Brother's Best Friend Novella

Deck the Halls: A Brother's Best Friend Novella

www.ingramcontent.com/pod-product-compliance
Lightning Source LLC
LaVergne TN
LVHW051002080826
845145LV00009B/2418

9781735530239